They heard something. A grunt. Then a growl. The sasquatch was nearby. Something snapped loudly—a piece of metal, maybe. Noah peered out between two panels: the sasquatch had broken a spring, knocking a yellow duck to the ground. The beast took a few steps, grabbed a happy blue whale, and hurled it into the air. Noah pulled back his head. The sasquatch was coming their way.

Noah stared into Ella's eyes and mouthed, *Don't move.*

THE SECRET ZOO

TRAPS AND SPECTERS

BRYAN CHICK

GREENWILLOW BOOKS
An Imprint of HarperCollinsPublishers

The Secret Zoo: Traps and Specters
Copyright © 2012 by Bryan Chick
First published in 2012 in hardcover; first paperback edition, 2013.

The text of this book is set in Arrus BT.
Book design by Paul Zakris

Library of Congress Cataloging-in-Publication Data
Chick, Bryan.
Traps and specters / by Bryan Chick.
pages cm.—(The secret zoo ; 4)
"Greenwillow Books."
Summary: "On Halloween night, the scouts, along with their Descender allies, must battle terrifying sasquatches at their own elementary school. Little do they know, the sasquatches are merely the bait to a trap. DeGraff captures three of the Descenders and drags them into a frightening, off-limits sector of The Secret Zoo. Meanwhile, Noah and his friends must protect two of their animal allies from police officers who are convinced that they are dangerous animals on the rampage. Will the scouts be able to save their friends in time, both animal and human?"—Provided by publisher.
ISBN 978-0-06-219222-6 (hardback)
ISBN 978-0-06-219223-3 (pbk.)
[1. Zoos—Fiction. 2. Zoo animals—Fiction.
3. Secret societies—Fiction. 4. Human-animal relationships—Fiction.
5. Sasquatch—Fiction. 6. Friendship—Fiction.] I. Title.
PZ7.C4336Tr 2012 [Fic]—dc23 2012018010

16 OPM 10 9 8 7 6 5 4 3
First Edition

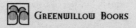
GREENWILLOW BOOKS

⊸✹ CHAPTER 1 ✹⊸

INTO THE SHADOWS

He moved across the Clarksville Zoo. In the midnight sky, clouds slipped across a bright moon, claiming its light. Throughout the zoo, animals slept. Most of them. Others were on patrol. The man lifted his pale face and spotted two koalas clinging to tree branches, their dark, beady eyes turned to him. He saw owls, orangutans, and a red panda chewing on a bamboo leaf. They were watching for the man the Secret Society feared most. The Shadowist. DeGraff.

He sneered. The animals were stupid. All of them.

Toward the middle of the grounds, he stepped into

Flamingo Fountain, a glass building in which a marble fountain sprayed streams of water straight up. The drone and splash of the artificial spring grew louder and louder until it became the only sound. He walked through a cloud of cool mist, squinting. Then he stepped back outside, the door easing shut behind him.

He had a heavy pack on each of his shoulders, and as he rounded Metr-APE-olis he arched his back in different ways to adjust them. Near Koala Kastle, he spotted a few otters posted in the bushes. Their twitching snouts sniffed the air and traced his passage. He wondered if any of the Descenders could see him. Sam, Solana, Tameron, Hannah—were any of them watching?

The shadowy rooftops of the surrounding neighborhood resembled the peaks of tiny, black pyramids. Smoke streamed from their chimneys, and a few large antennas looked like the cleanly picked bones of strange animals. He spotted a monkey jumping from one house to another. A police-monkey, on patrol. It would spend all night secretly leaping across the rooftops in its tireless circle of the zoo.

The man reached the west entrance, where a bulb buzzed overhead and a cone of light fell across a concrete path that led to a small, wrought-iron gate. He glanced over his shoulder and slipped into a booth beside the path. Inside, a guard sat in a chair, his feet propped up on a small desk. He was gnawing on the end of a toothpick, rolling it across his lips. The two exchanged nods. Then the man carefully set one of his backpacks at the feet of the guard, who quickly looked down at it.

"This it?" the guard asked.

The man nodded.

"When?"

"Soon. In the meantime, just make sure no one finds it."

"You got it, boss."

Their conversation ended, and the guard began again to noisily pick at his teeth. The man stared him up and down and decided he didn't look much different. Not yet.

The man moved to a window and scanned the trees along the perimeter wall. Somewhere in them, animals were posted, hoping to spot the Shadowist advancing on the zoo. In almost a century, it had never happened. And except for the few times Noah and his friends had glimpsed him, he'd never been seen at all.

The man intended to change this. Tonight.

He reached around and patted his remaining backpack, ensuring everything was there. It was. He turned, slipped out of the booth, and quietly stepped through the gate. Now outside the zoo, he sank into the cover of the trees along the concrete wall, dead leaves crinkling beneath his weight. He hunkered in the thick underbrush and eased the backpack off his shoulders.

He waited. He watched the treetops. Nothing stirred. He was certain he hadn't been seen by any of the animals.

A line of bats flew past, but he had no reason to worry about them. They'd see him, but they wouldn't notice him.

He waited a few minutes, then dumped the contents of his pack. Seeing them lying there—realizing what they were—he suddenly became nervous. He glanced all around to reassure himself that he was alone.

On the ground lay a trench coat, gloves, and a hat.

First he gathered up the coat, which was long and leather. He stood, fed his arms through its sleeves, and let its length spill down his legs. Next he donned the gloves, finger by finger. Finally he put on the hat. It was a fedora with a tall crown and a wide brim that bent down over his face.

The man pulled up his collar, tipped the hat down to mask his eyes, then fled, his open trench coat fluttering behind him like a cape. He went swiftly from one point to the next, keeping cover under the trees and in the deeper shadows. They were watching, of this he was certain. From the trees, the rooftops, the sky, the ground—owls and bats and tarsiers.

He dashed across a backyard and hurdled a short fence, his long coat slipping across the sharp pickets. He dodged behind a tree and pressed his back flat against the trunk.

He listened for movement in the treetops. Nothing. He pushed off and hurried across the lawn, the edges of his coat snapping. He sank into the shadow of a small shed. From beneath the curved brim of his hat, he turned his eyes to the star-spotted sky. No owls, no bats.

Something moved on a rooftop, two houses down. He peered out and tried to extract shapes from the darkness. Smoke plumed from a chimney, tree branches swayed, billowy clouds drifted across the sky, but nothing else.

Then, suddenly, two silhouettes rose on the rooftop. Two creatures—police-monkeys, no doubt—charged to the edge of the house and lunged six or seven feet to the next one, their dark forms falling into the shadows there.

He slipped inside the shed and eased the door shut, careful not to make a sound. He wrinkled his nose at the stinging smells: fertilizer, paints, and rust. The small space was silent—no wind, no creaking branches, no drone of faraway cars. He leaned toward a small window and peered out. After a few minutes, the monkeys rose and bounded to the next house, disappearing again. Several minutes later, they rose, ran forward, and jumped to the next roof.

He smiled. It was too easy to fool the Secret Society.

Of course it helped that he knew their plan.

He waited a few more minutes, allowing time for the monkeys to get farther down the neighborhood, then slipped out the door. He headed across the backyard, keeping again to the shadows. He ran between two houses and ducked behind a hedge in a front yard. In all directions, the treetops were perfectly still—he hadn't been seen.

He ran from the bushes and dashed across the street. In the new yard, he set his back against a tree and scanned the treetops again. No movement of any kind.

He turned to the house. Two stories high and made of brick, it stood behind bushes that were groomed into different shapes. A porch lay beneath a wide picture window with closed curtains. He ran across the lawn and jumped onto the stoop. Leaning forward, he peered through a slit between the curtains. The flickering light of a television revealed a girl sitting on a couch, alone.

He smiled a wicked smile. Then he lifted his gloved hand and pecked with a fingertip against the glass.

≈❧ CHAPTER 2 ❧≈
OUT OF THE SHADOWS

Ella's eyes jumped from the TV to the front door. Had she heard something? Because her mom was playing cards at Mrs. Carson's, Ella was alone in the house.

The sound came again, a simple *tap*.

She swatted the television remote like a bug and the room fell into darkness. The new silence seemed to have an actual presence—a ghost that had crept in near her.

"Hello?" she asked.

Tap!

She looked out the picture window and realized the curtains weren't completely drawn. Peering through the gap, she saw nothing but a long sliver of the night. Was someone out there? Megan? Perhaps Marlo or another animal from the Secret Zoo?

She bounced off the couch, stepped into the front hall, and yanked the door open. The only thing separating her from the outside was a flimsy screen door. The cold air washed across her body.

"Meg—that you?"

No answer.

She took a deep breath and the cold rushed into her lungs. She cracked open the creaky screen door and peered across the porch. No one.

"Hello? Marlo?"

Wind rustled leaves on the ground.

As she stepped out, the screen door slamming behind her made her jump. The cold of the concrete rose through the rubbery soles of her fluffy pink slippers. The wind collected in the cavity of the porch, whipping her pony-tail about. She wrapped her arms over her chest, moved to a place with a good view of her yard, and stared into the darkness.

"Hello?" she asked again.

Nothing. Just leaves tumbling and grass bending under the breath of the sky.

Across the street, a treetop began to shake. Ella peered at it but couldn't see much in its inky web of branches.

Then something small shot through the air and disappeared into the tree's silhouette. The limb became still, then the *something small* flew back out and etched a path through the sky in the direction of the Clarksville Zoo.

Ella felt a fresh chill work across her body—a chill that this time hadn't been brought on by the cold. She knew the thing headed toward the zoo was an owl. And she knew what this meant.

As she turned to rush inside, she saw movement out of the corner of her eye, and she stopped. Someone had just stepped out from behind a tall evergreen, a man in a billowy trench coat with the collar turned up. He wore boots and gloves and a hat with a wide, circular brim.

The Shadowist.

After tapping on her window to lead her outside, he'd hidden behind the tree. Now he stood with his back to the street, his arms down, his legs braced far apart, his face masked in the deep shadows of his hat. In the wind, his open coat rolled and snapped.

Ella looked down her neighborhood. How long would it take for the owl to reach the zoo? For the guards and Descenders to arrive? She turned back to DeGraff. Her heart banged against her chest. She couldn't bear the silence any longer.

"What . . . what do you want?"

The Shadowist simply stood in the dark swirl of his

coat, saying nothing. His open hands clenched. A gust of wind scattered hundreds of leaves, whirling some around his boots.

High above the street, a line of bats flew by. But they didn't stop, or slow, or move in a new direction. It was like their echolocation had failed to detect DeGraff.

Just as Ella thought this strange, the Shadowist suddenly broke into a run, straight at her. But before he could reach the porch, he fell headfirst into the bushes, his trench coat flapping over his head. Branches broke off and whirled through the air.

Ella looked down and saw what had happened. Prairie dogs. At least a dozen were scattered about. They'd tripped DeGraff after springing up from a tunnel somewhere beneath her yard.

Before DeGraff could push himself out of the bushes, the prairie dogs jumped onto him, sinking their teeth into his trench coat. When he finally stood, they slid off his coat, their teeth ripping through the leather, and struck the ground. They quickly found their bearings and lunged back at him, biting into his pant legs. DeGraff snatched a prairie dog by its stubby tail and threw it toward the street. He grabbed a second one by the scruff of its neck and hurled it aside. Ella stood frozen in place, unsure if she should help her animal friends or retreat into her house. DeGraff spun around and then stopped moving, his gaze locked on something in the distance on the street. Ella peered out and saw three figures charging toward her house: two zoo guards and Solana.

As DeGraff broke toward one side of the house, a prairie dog charged straight at him. Ella instantly recognized him as P-Dog, the chubbiest one in the small coterie. Before he could attack, DeGraff kicked out his foot and P-Dog flew through the air onto Ella's porch, his body crashing hard against the brick wall of the house.

"*No!*" Ella screamed.

P-Dog lay perfectly still. Ella dropped to her knees and touched his side to ensure he was breathing. When her hand grazed his front left leg, he yipped in pain. He tried to get up and couldn't.

"It's okay, P," Ella said as she stroked his side. "You're okay."

She looked up to see DeGraff fleeing between her house and her neighbor's, the prairie dogs giving chase. Several houses away, Solana and the two guards veered onto the neighbors' yards, hopping hedges and dodging parked cars. When they reached Ella's property, they followed DeGraff and the other animals. Within seconds, everyone was gone.

Everyone but P-Dog.

She glanced all around. Had anyone seen anything? The windows of nearby houses were dark and empty.

P-Dog tried to stand and collapsed. He lay on the porch, his side rising and falling with each rushed breath. He was badly hurt, but Ella wasn't sure how to help him.

Headlights suddenly streaked across the houses on the opposite side of the street as a car rounded a turn. The moon revealed a white minivan—her mother's car, only five or six houses down.

In a panic, Ella scooped up P-Dog, opened the door a crack, and squirmed back into the house. Her mother's van pulled into the drive and light burst along the edges of the picture window curtain. The engine fell silent, then the driver's door squealed open and slammed shut. Her mother's heels clicked against the sidewalk, louder and louder until they finally stopped. Ms. Jones was on the porch.

Ella looked into her arms and locked stares with P-Dog. Then her gaze moved to the doorknob and she glimpsed a tiny image of her surprised self in the curve of its shiny brass—eyes wide, lips arched in a small oval.

She stood frozen in place, the upstairs staircase to her left, the living room to her right, and a long hallway leading to the kitchen directly behind her. As she heard the muffled clatter of her mother's keys, she retreated down the hall. When she tried to round the corner, her foot slipped, causing two things to go airborne: one of her fluffy pink slippers and P-Dog. Both sailed across the kitchen and banged into the base of the cupboards. Ella lay on her back, her limbs and emotions in separate tangles.

The doorknob rattled and spun and Ms. Jones stepped into the house, her greeting a strange sort of song: *"Elll—lllaa! I'm hooommme!"*

❦ CHAPTER 3 ❦

PROTECTING P-DOG

Ms. Jones didn't immediately see Ella. As the door closed, she continued her semi-song: *"Elll-lllaaa."* Ella heard her mother drop her purse on a bench and strip off her jacket, which she flung over the staircase rail. As she turned to the hallway, she gasped and her shoes squeaked to a stop.

"Oh my . . . You scared me half to— What are you *doing*?" She seemed to realize Ella's predicament. "Are you hurt?"

Still on her back, Ella lifted her head and stared around the kitchen. Expecting to find P-Dog, she spotted only her fuzzy slipper. It lay like a half-squashed pink gerbil.

She scanned the reaches of the room—beside the fridge and beneath the overhang of the cabinets. There was no sign of her animal friend.

"Ella—answer me!"

Ella looked up and saw her mother now looming above her. From Ella's vantage point, her mother's body was totally out of proportion. Even her nose looked strange, like something she could reach up and detach, set on the countertop beside her cell phone and car keys.

Ella jumped to her feet and dusted off her pajamas. "Just my feelings." She turned and retrieved her slipper from the kitchen. As she sank her foot back into its fuzzy warmth, her mother started patting her down.

"What happened?"

"I was walking to open the door and my slippers tripped me up. No biggie." Scanning the kitchen again for P-Dog, Ella quickly switched the subject: "How was your card game?"

Instead of answering, Ms. Jones continued to study her daughter for signs of something wrong. Suspicion curled up one of her eyebrows.

"Ma?"

Finally, her mother let down her guard. "Not bad, I guess." She walked over to the fridge and rummaged inside it. "You'll never guess what happened to Mrs. Carson last week!"

"What's that?" Ella said, feigning interest as best she could.

Her mother pushed aside the ketchup, the mayonnaise, a clear container full of goop which might have been days-old stew. "She bowls, you know . . . with Mrs. Anderson and a couple other ladies. Well . . . last week . . ."

Her voice became a murmur as Ella divided her attention between it and the whereabouts of P-Dog. As Ella searched from the corners of her eyes, she caught occasional words: ". . . Mrs. Baker, that new lady down the street . . ." and ". . . decided to come along . . ." and "Ella! Are you listening?" Ella nodded and curled the ends of her lips up.

Ms. Jones closed the fridge, a few slips of lunch meat drooping over her fingers, and headed to the bread basket. Ella took the opportunity to hurry into the connecting great room. She began checking behind the furniture, mouthing *P-Dog!* over and over. After a minute or two, Ms. Jones poked her head into the room and Ella jerked upright and fixed her attention back on her mother, who was waving a spoon in the air, saying something about Mrs. Baker dropping a bowling ball on someone's foot. Her mother laughed, then her head retreated into the kitchen as she returned to her work on her sandwich.

Ella peered under the couch. The only thing beneath it was the pink headband she'd lost about a year ago. It lay there covered in dust like a half-buried treasure in an archeological dig.

Her mother stepped into the dining room, this time carrying a plate and a glass of juice. She was talking about someone's swollen toe—a toe that the bowling ball had undoubtedly landed on. She took a seat facing Ella at the dining room table, lifted the sandwich, and tore off a bite. She chewed for a few seconds, then returned to her story. Ella smiled and nodded in the places she guessed appropriate.

From the same doorway that Ms. Jones had just stepped through, P-Dog suddenly poked his head into the room, his twitching nose pulling scents out of the air. Ella went rigid with fear. Her mother, sensing something wrong, followed Ella's gaze, but before she could spot P-Dog, the wounded prairie dog hobbled forward and disappeared beneath the table, right in front of her feet.

Ms. Jones turned back to Ella. Through a mouthful of food, she asked again if Ella was *sure* she hadn't hurt herself. Ella nodded. The way her mother waited to chew her food made Ella nervous. Finally, Ms. Jones snapped her jaws back into action. After a swallow, she continued her story, in which the big toe was now swollen to the size of a mature walnut.

Ella pretended to listen, a forced expression of interest on her face. Her gaze repeatedly dropped down to where

P-Dog was now sitting, bug-eyed and jittery. After a few seconds, the unthinkable happened. Ms. Jones stretched out her legs and accidentally bumped P-Dog with her foot. When she dropped her head to peek beneath the table, she discovered the prairie dog lying completely still.

Ella gasped. She took a step forward and stopped. There was nothing she could do. They'd been caught, and now the Secret Zoo would be discovered.

After what seemed a long time, Ms. Jones sat upright and casually returned to the business of chewing her food. She swallowed and said, "All these stuffed animals—when are you ever going to get rid of them?" She sipped her juice. "Can't you at least pick them up?"

Ella smiled weakly. "Sorry, Mom."

Ms. Jones took the last bite of her sandwich. "Isn't that funny?"

Ella thought that her mom was referring to P-Dog, then realized she was talking about her story. With a nod, she smiled her big, fake, rubbery smile again.

Ms. Jones rose from the table and carried her empty plate back into the kitchen, saying, "C'mon—pick that up. I don't want to see those things lying around."

"Sorry, Mom."

From the kitchen, Ms. Jones craned her neck back into the dining room. "And since when are you so polite? Stop—it's making me nervous."

Careful not to speak and invite more conversation, Ella simply continued to hold up her smile.

Ms. Jones grunted and slipped back into the kitchen. When her plate banged into the sink and the faucet spilled its noisy water, Ella reached beneath the dining room table and swept up P-Dog. She fled the room and dashed up the stairs, her fluffy slippers two pink blurs over the carpet.

Just after midnight, at least an hour after Ms. Jones had fallen asleep, Ella was in her room, sitting on her bed in front of the window, staring out into the night. As usual, she couldn't see any tarsiers posted in the trees. She wondered if DeGraff had been captured—if Solana and the zoo guards had managed to get to him. Hope surged through her. The thing the Secret Society feared most—the Shadowist getting back to the magic of the Secret Zoo—might have ended tonight.

Ella turned to P-Dog, who was perched on his hind legs beside her. She wasn't sure what was wrong with him, but his side was swollen and he was having trouble walking. "P . . . I don't want to let you go—not tonight, not the way you are. The last thing I need to find on my way to school tomorrow is you squashed on the road, tire tracks across your face. In the morning . . . we'll get you back then."

The prairie dog looked up at Ella, his eyes gleaming like black marbles, and sniffed the air near her face.

Ella already had a plan. It involved the prairie dog tunnels that extended from the Grottoes and ran through her neighborhood—the ones the prairie dogs had emerged from to attack DeGraff tonight. She had no idea where the tunnels came out into her yard, so she couldn't risk having P-Dog roam around her property in plain view of her mother or anyone else. But she did know where they opened into a hidden spot in Noah's backyard. Every morning, Ella walked to school with the other scouts. If she could release P-Dog by the tunnel in Noah's yard, he could trek the short distance back to the zoo, even with his injuries. She just needed to figure out how to get P-Dog across the neighborhood without him being seen.

Thinking about this, Ella stared into her closet and spotted her backpack. She pointed to it and said, "What do you think, P?"

P-Dog followed her stare. After a few seconds he turned back to Ella, his eyes wide with concern. He yipped once, a bit defiantly, Ella thought.

"If you've got a better idea, I'd love to hear it."

Seeming to consider this, he tipped his head one way, then another. After a few seconds, he looked away.

"I didn't think so."

Ella turned back to the dark streets. Her mind replayed

the incident on her front porch. She kept imagining DeGraff, the wide brim of his hat, his upturned collar, his long trench coat. Why had he come to her door? She wondered again if he had been caught. If not, would he be back again tonight? The thought sent waves of terror through her. An hour passed. Then another. Near two o'clock in the morning, she finally dropped the blinds and fell into bed, lying on her side. P-Dog curled up against her stomach, and she rested her palm on him.

"Thanks, P . . . for being there tonight, I mean."

P-Dog sniffed her hand, his puny nose dotting moisture on her skin.

Believing she'd never relax, Ella closed her eyes and immediately drifted off. The world of reality became the world of her dreams, two places divided by a line that seemed to be thinning more each day.

CHAPTER 4

PACKING P-DOG

Ella woke to her alarm clock. Grumbling, she rolled over, pinching something between her stomach and the mattress—a *something* that gave a squeaky *yip*! She threw herself to the edge of the bed and saw a small animal lying in her pink sheets. P-Dog. It looked like he was resting in a pink pasture. Memories of the previous night swarmed into her head.

A muffled voice came from out in the hall: "Ella?" Then knuckles rapped the bedroom door. "You okay in there?"

Ella flung the blankets over P-Dog and jumped to the

floor. "Don't move," she warned the pink bump on her bed.

Her bedroom door swung open and in walked her mother. "I made waffles. Hurry up and get them before they get cold."

"Thanks, Ma."

Her mother backed out of the room, and once her footsteps had faded away, Ella softly closed the door and hurried back to her bed, where P-Dog was squirming around. She threw off the blankets, scooped him up in one arm, then gently placed him into the closet on a pile of half-folded sweaters. He peered out from the colorful cotton and yipped again.

"Sorry, P. But you have to stay here till I'm done eating."

Ella shut the closet door, left her room, and hurried down the hall. In the dining room, she dropped into her seat and scarfed up her waffles, her mother grimacing more than once at Ella's overloaded cheeks.

Back upstairs, she eased open her closet. P-Dog shot her a scornful look and waded out from the spill he'd made of the sweaters. She wriggled into her clothes, grabbed her backpack, and pried it open like the mouth of an alligator. She stuffed her zoo uniform inside, then held the opening toward P-Dog. "Here."

The prairie dog sniffed curiously at the bag, then backed away.

"C'mon—what's the matter?" She poked her face into the opening. "Okay, so it stinks a little. It doubles as my soccer bag, you know."

P-Dog took another step back.

"Look, it's only for a few minutes. Just until we get to Noah's."

P-Dog inched forward and sniffed the air a second time. As he did, Ella lifted him by his belly, carried him into the bag, and zipped it shut. P-Dog yipped once and turned in circles, his body making a lump under the nylon.

"Sorry, P," Ella said as she stood and eased one strap over her shoulder. "It'll just be a few minutes, I promise."

P-Dog wriggled into a comfortable position and became still. Ella stomped down the stairs, set the backpack onto a chair near the front door, and put on her jacket and earmuffs. After hoisting P-Dog onto her back again, she called, "Bye, Mom!" and pushed out onto the porch. It was pouring rain.

"Great."

The door creaked open and her mother's hand appeared, clutching an umbrella. "Here." Then she stated the obvious: "It's raining."

Ella took the umbrella, sprang it open, and headed out, a scowl on her face. As she crossed her yard, wet leaves clung to her shoes like giant leeches. P-Dog kept squirming around in her pack, forcing the straps off her shoulders. "Knock it off, dork," she kept saying.

As she headed down Jenkins Street toward Noah's house, a car approached, its headlights causing the raindrops to sparkle. It slowed to a crawl beside her and the driver's window dropped, revealing Mrs. Nowicki, Noah and Megan's mom. The wind tossed her curly, uncombed hair.

"C'mon," Mrs. Nowicki said. She tipped her head toward the backseat. "Hop in."

Ella's heart sank. "Huh?"

"I'm not about to let you kids walk to school in the middle of a hurricane."

The back door swung open to reveal Richie, the cold, moist air fogging his giant glasses. He scooted his skinny rear end over, making room for Ella. Beside him sat Megan. In the front passenger seat was Noah.

"I . . ." Ella said. "I don't know. I kind of . . . I kind of feel like walking."

"You mean *swimming*?" Richie said.

Feeling P-Dog shifting in her backpack, Ella lowered her eyebrows and tried to communicate her concern to Richie. "It's just . . . today's a *really, really* bad day for a ride."

"Ella," Mrs. Nowicki said, "if I let you walk in this rain while driving all your friends, your mother will never speak to me again. Now get in."

Ella waited. She wanted to walk away but knew Mrs. Nowicki would come after her.

Richie patted the open seat beside him.

She slumped her shoulders and let the backpack slip down her arms. She plopped onto the seat, cradled the bag in her lap, and closed the door. Mrs. Nowicki sped off, her wipers groaning.

Richie looked at Ella's full bag. "Man—what do you have in that thing?"

Ella shot him a wry look. "A prairie dog."

Believing it was a joke, Mrs. Nowicki chuckled.

But she was the only one.

ᕷ CHAPTER 5 ᕷ

P-Dog Gets Schooled

"You're kidding, right?" Richie said as the scouts headed up one of the long, winding paths of the concrete courtyard before their school's front entrance. Clarksville Elementary had a main building with three wings. Each wing housed two grade levels. Ten years ago, the old school building had been demolished to make room for a larger one, parts of which—the gym, the cafeteria, the media center—were over two stories high.

"Tell me you're not serious," Richie pleaded. "Tell me P-Dog's not really in your backpack right now."

Ella shifted the backpack on her shoulders. "Nope, no joke."

Richie touched Ella's backpack, and when something wriggled, he pulled his hand back.

"She's not kidding, guys. I just felt P-Dog's head. Or his butt. It was something round, anyway. And it was moving."

The friends pushed through the front doors of Clarksville Elementary, leaving behind the rain and a lineup of buses. They moved down one of the wings and stopped at Megan's locker. As Megan spun through her combination, Ella briefed them on the previous night. When she mentioned her confrontation with DeGraff, everyone's mouths dropped open.

"DeGraff!" Megan gasped. She peered over both her shoulders to make certain no one could hear them. "In your front yard . . . DeGraff! I can't . . . I can't *believe* this."

"Well, believe it, sister," Ella said as she shifted her backpack again. "He was knocking on my front door like a Girl Scout with cookies."

Ella quickly told them the rest of the story: DeGraff, the prairie dogs, Solana and the zoo guards, P-Dog and how he'd wound up getting a ride in her backpack.

"Not good," Richie said, shaking his head. "And I'm talking in a really major way."

Megan shut her door and they walked the short way to Noah's locker. As Noah hung up his jacket, he said, "Okay, don't freak out. We have crosstraining after school. We just need to make it through the day—that shouldn't be too hard, right?" As he banged the steel door shut, the morning bell rang, scattering kids toward their classrooms. The scouts headed to Richie's locker.

"What am I supposed to do with P-Dog?" Ella asked. "Put him in my locker?"

"Not a good idea," Richie said. "You can hardly breathe in those things—trust me, I know." Richie was referring to how Wide Walt, the school bully, would sometimes squeeze him into his locker and shut the door when teachers weren't around.

Megan gasped. "He'd suffocate!"

Richie opened his locker. The inside walls bulged outward in the general shape of his body. When trapped in the steely confines, Richie knew how to wriggle into a comfortable position until someone, usually one of the scouts, set him free. Closing his door, Richie said, "Take your backpack with you. Keep it close—under your desk or something."

"Are you nuts!" Ella said. "How am I supposed—"

But Richie and Noah were already walking away. As the boys turned to their open classroom door, Noah looked back to Ella and shrugged, saying, "What else are we supposed to do?"

"Great . . ." Ella said. She led Megan down the hall, opened her locker, and fed her belongings inside—

everything but her backpack. Then the two girls squirmed through the thinning crowd of students and walked into Room 112, their split-grade class.

Mrs. Simons was rambling on about decimals and place values, scrawling large numbers across the whiteboard and dropping dots at their feet. Ella couldn't have cared less. All she could think about was the backpack beneath her chair. She kept touching it with her feet, each time breathing a sigh of relief. Though she knew Megan was watching the bag from across the room, she couldn't help but fear P-Dog would find a way to manipulate the zipper open and sneak out for a stroll.

Trying to think of something other than P-Dog, Ella looked over at the bulletin board beside the Word Wall. There were announcements about different things: a lost jacket, a lost necklace, the school play tryouts. Two posters were tacked to it. One promoted a reading campaign called "Reading Is Your Key," and the other advertised the school Halloween party, a green-faced witch with a hooked nose saying, "Come to Clarksville Elementary's Halloween Bash! You'll have a *ghoul* time!"

The Halloween poster reminded Ella of DeGraff again, the way he had stood among the swirl of leaves in her front yard, his body a silhouette against the night, his fingers curled into half-fists, the wind beating his trench coat against his boots. The fright of Halloween had come early to Ella's household—and this year that fright was real.

Ella turned away from the bulletin board and watched the second hand of the clock sweep around in its slow, endless circle. Mrs. Simons changed subjects. History, maybe. Or government. When you were worried about a live zoo animal in your backpack, all the subjects seemed the same.

About an hour into the school day, Peter Wilkins approached the front of the room and accidentally hooked his foot in the strap of Ella's backpack, slinging it across the aisle. It came to a stop against the leg of Mackenzie McCarthy's chair, and everyone stared at it for what it was: something-that-did-not-belong. The only sound became that of Tana Quinn wetly chomping her gum.

Flushed with embarrassment and fear, Ella reached out into the aisle with her foot and snagged back the pack. She tucked it neatly beneath her chair and did her best to ignore Peter's dirty look.

When the students broke for recess two hours later, Ella took her backpack. Outside, the scouts headed toward the Monster Dome, avoiding the puddles left behind by the morning storm. On the climber's steel bars, a bunch of second graders were hanging upside down, their faces looking like turnips, red and swollen. The scouts gathered in a quiet area far behind the action.

Noah gestured toward Ella's backpack. "Everything okay so far?"

Ella zipped open her bag. P-Dog poked out his snout and gave the playground air a curious sniff, looking no worse for wear. Ella quickly palmed his head and pushed him back inside. "Sorry, P," she said as she sealed the bag.

"I just thought of something," Richie said. "What if P-Dog has to go to the bathroom?" When the scouts gave him blank stares, he felt the need to elaborate. "You know . . . the number two type."

Ella said, "Then I guess things are going to get a little stinky."

For the rest of recess, the scouts listened again to Ella tell her story of the previous night. Despite all they'd been through with the Secret Zoo, it still seemed unreal—DeGraff in her front yard, Solana and the guards chasing him down their streets. When the bell rang, the four friends merged into a crowd of children headed indoors. In the hallways, sounds echoed off the steel lockers and concrete walls. Ella made her way into class and slipped her backpack under her desk once more. She felt the bag shift as P-Dog squirmed into a new position.

Once everyone had settled in at their desks, Mrs. Simons started talking about something. Ella couldn't pay attention. Like a sports team with a narrow lead, she only cared about beating the clock.

When the class was dismissed for lunch, Ella jumped from her desk and scooped up the backpack. She followed Megan down to the cafeteria line, paid two dollars for a slimy concoction involving noodles and clumpy gravy, then took a seat beside Richie and Noah, where she put her bag on the table beside her tray.

Then, not a minute later, the worst thing that could happen happened.

❧ CHAPTER 6 ❧

WIDE WALT ARRIVES

"What's up, *dorks*."

The voice, deep and menacing, had come from Wide Walter White, the worst bully in Clarksville Elementary. From between two long rows of tables, Walt strutted toward the scouts, his elbows batting the heads of a few seated students. Dave and Doug, his two cronies, followed and glared all around, daring anyone to attempt eye contact.

"Great . . ." Megan groaned as she steered her attention back to her tray. "Here comes bonehead."

Walt continued toward them, his wide shoulders

swaying. When one student was struck by Walt's elbow, his glasses fell off and plopped into his wet pile of noodles. When another student was bumped, his spork missed his mouth and instead jabbed his ear. Noah glanced around and saw there wasn't a single adult in sight.

"The Action Dorks," Walt slurred, as if he were talking around a mouthful of pebbles. When he neared the scouts, his gaze fell to Ella's backpack. "What's in the bag?"

Noah watched his friends tense up. It was Ella who answered—a bit too quickly and defensively, Noah thought.

"Nothing."

"Nothing? What kind of an idiot walks around carrying a bag of nothing?" Dave and Doug nodded once, twice, three times. Noah thought they looked like bobble heads, the kind you stick on the dashboard of a car.

"Walt . . ." Ella said, "your head is a bag of nothing and *you* still carry it around."

Walt's eyes opened so big that Noah could actually see their roundness.

"Talk a walk, White," Ella said. "You're blocking our light, you gargantuan oaf."

Walt's back stiffened. He studied the nearby students to calculate how many had witnessed the insult. Then he slowly drew down his eyelids and leaned so close to Ella that she could have puckered up and planted a kiss on his lips.

"What—did—you—just—say?"

Ella locked her stare on his. A fourth grader at the next table gasped. Another student began to whimper.

"Okay," Walt said with a sneer. "I'll walk. But not without *this*." With a clean jerk of his arm, he seized Ella's backpack and slung it over his shoulder.

The scouts jumped up. Noah reached across the table, spilling his chocolate milk. Ella swiped at her pack and missed, her fingertips grazing Walt's shirt.

"Whooaaa!" Walt said, his voice quivering with laughter. "What do you got in this thing?"

"Give it back, Walt!" Megan shouted. "Give it back *now*!"

"Or what? What are you twerps going to do?"

Ella swiped at her backpack a second time, missing completely. Walt jumped back and allowed his friends to step in front of him like a shield. When Noah again reached across the table, Walt snickered. He juggled his stare between Noah and Ella, saying, *"Maaaan* . . . whatever you dorks got in here, it must be good." He fumbled for the zipper.

Ella lunged forward, but Walt's cronies held her back. She reached around Doug, her open hand sweeping through the air. "Let—go—of—me!" she said, her words snapping out one at a time.

"Get your hands off her!" Richie hollered. He reached around Ella and shoved Doug, who didn't budge.

Just as Noah was about to yell for help, Walt unzipped the backpack and, without looking, plunged his hand inside. He immediately squealed, dropped the bag to the floor, and stared with wide eyes at several dots of blood on his finger.

Ella reached around the legs of Walt's friends and snatched up her pack. She pitched it across the table into the open arms of Noah, who zipped it, then tossed it over to Megan, who was farthest from Walt.

"You *freak*!" Walt poked his finger into his mouth to suck off the blood, then pulled it back out. "What the heck's in that thing?"

Dave and Doug backed away from Ella until they bumped against Walt.

"Not telling," Ella said. "But for fifty bucks, you can have the antidote."

Walt's eyes widened with worry. It was obvious he believed her, at least a little.

From across the cafeteria, a voice rang out: *"White!"*

A hundred heads turned, and the room fell to silence. Standing at the end of the tables was Mr. Kershen, the toughest teacher in Clarksville Elementary. He marched between the benches and stopped at the scene, his hands propped on his hips.

"You guys haven't learned to get along yet?"

Walt uncorked his finger from his mouth with a slight popping sound. He shook his bleeding fingertip toward Ella and said, "That freak . . . she's got something in her bag! Something that—"

"You mind telling me what you were doing with her backpack?"

Walt's eyes shifted as he searched for a good lie. "I . . . I thought she took my library book."

Mr. Kershen's face fell in a frown. He hooked his finger inside his shirt collar and pulled it away from his neck. "You got to be kidding me." As he spoke, his mustache rolled like a wounded caterpillar. "White—the last time you checked out a book it was a *movie*."

"But . . . Mr. Kershen . . . I . . ."

"C'mon . . ." He grabbed Walt's arm and led him down the aisle between the tables. "To the principal's office."

Walt's friends, suddenly unsure about everything, dashed out of sight.

The scouts dropped into their seats and Megan slid the backpack over to Ella. Within seconds the normal cafeteria activity resumed. Among the chatter of the students, Richie found it safe to talk.

"'Gargantuan oaf'?" he said to Ella. "Where in the world did that come from?"

Ella shrugged. "I guess stress brings out my vocabulary."

Noah turned and watched Mr. Kershen escort Walt from the cafeteria. This was the third time in two years that Walt had gotten in trouble after an altercation with the scouts.

The thought made Noah very nervous.

CHAPTER 7

Retrieving Richie

When the final bell sounded that day, students poured out of their classrooms, running, hollering, and laughing. The twang of flimsy locker doors filled the air, and a few wads of paper sailed overhead. As Noah and Richie headed through the commotion, they kept a careful watch for Wide Walt. They'd learned that Walt hadn't been sent home after the incident in the cafeteria. This meant he could be prowling the halls, looking to retaliate.

Noah squirmed through the students to get to his locker, and Richie continued down the hall to his own.

After spinning through his combination, Noah opened the door and pulled out his jacket. Megan and Ella approached, their coats and backpacks already on. Ella was wearing her pink earmuffs and Megan her fleece headband.

"We ready to roll?" Ella asked as she pulled her gloves tight.

Noah nodded. He slipped on his jacket and his backpack, then closed his locker. "P-Dog okay?"

"I guess. I can feel him moving around."

Walt and his two cronies suddenly charged past on their way to the main entrance. Walt was laughing and gleefully pushing kids aside.

"What's that thug so happy about?" Ella asked. "He finally learn the alphabet?"

Noah shrugged. He stared in the direction from which Walt had come and couldn't spot Richie in the thinning crowd. But on the floor by Richie's locker lay his jacket and backpack.

"Uh-oh," Noah said.

Ella followed Noah's gaze. "Did Walt just make a sardine out of Richie again?"

Noah shook his head in disgust. "C'mon . . . let's go get him."

The three of them hurried down the hall, weaving through kids. When they reached Richie's locker,

Noah said, "You in there?"

A voice came through the vent at the top of the locker: "Alas, it is I."

Noah dialed in Richie's locker combination—each of the scouts kept it memorized for this exact situation. "You hurt?"

"Not really." Richie's voice was muffled and tinny. "It's actually quite comfortable in here."

Noah opened the door to see that Richie was turned half sideways, the curves of his skinny body fitted into permanent dents in the locker walls. His shoulders were slouched and his glasses were crooked. A few pens had fallen from his shirt pocket and lay on the steel floor.

Ella grabbed Richie's arms and yanked him out. She stared up the hall at the place Walt had been. "Someone really needs to lay out that clown!"

Richie bent over and collected his pens off the ground. "And, rest assured, that someone is *not* going to be me." He donned his jacket and backpack and closed the locker door. "Forget about him," Richie said as he made a move toward the exit. "We have more important things to worry about."

The scouts watched their friend walk off. After a few seconds, Noah said, "He's right. Walt's nothing next to DeGraff."

The girls nodded, and the four friends made their way through the crowd. Outside, they headed straight for the zoo, where crosstraining was scheduled to begin in just a few minutes at Koala Kastle.

CHAPTER 8

KOALA KASTLE

P-Dog stuck his head out from the backpack and sniffed the ground curiously, his whiskers twitching about. As he raised his snout to investigate the air, the wind lifted a leaf and dropped it on his furry face, startling him.

"Hurry up, P!" Ella said. *"Go!"*

He struggled out of the backpack and hobbled across the zoo lawn.

The scouts were at Little Dogs of the Prairie, the outdoor prairie dog exhibit in the Clarksville Zoo. It resembled a sandy prairie, one that was pitted with holes, and beneath it was a tunnel system that led first to the

Grottoes and then the Secret Zoo. The four friends were all alone—on such a cold weekday afternoon, the zoo was practically empty.

P-Dog crawled beneath the fence surrounding the exhibit and dove inside. He landed less than perfectly, his stomach smacking the ground. Several nearby prairie dogs sniffed his bad leg with concern, then led him to a tunnel hole, where he climbed inside and disappeared.

Ella grabbed her backpack and headed up the path. "C'mon—let's get our superhero costumes on."

On the day Mr. Darby, the leader of the Secret Zoo, had welcomed the scouts into the Secret Society as Crossers, Tank—Mr. Darby's right-hand man, a lead security guard at the Clarksville Zoo, and a good friend to the scouts—had given each of them a zoo uniform: an ugly shirt with oversized pockets and a long, stiff collar. The shirts disguised them as zoo volunteers. When the scouts cross-trained during the week, they changed in either their school bathroom or in BathZOOm, the nicest restroom in the Clarksville Zoo.

Everyone fell in line behind Ella. The day was cold, wet, and gray. A steady wind stripped leaves from half-barren trees and swept them off the ground into piles. With their necks and chins buried in their jackets, the scouts looked like turtles trying to duck into their shells.

"You know," Richie said, "some days it would be nice

just to go home from school and plop down on the couch."

After a few minutes, Ella turned onto the sidewalk leading to BathZOOm. Richie, his thoughts apparently more on getting out of the cold than on where he was going, followed Ella and Megan into the women's bathroom. As the door banged closed, Noah shook his head and began to count in his head: *One . . . two . . .*

"Richie!" screamed Ella and Megan.

The bathroom door flung open and out spilled Richie, saying, "Sorry, sorry, sorry!"

"Nice work," Noah teased.

The two boys headed into the proper bathroom, where they tossed their backpacks onto a bench and unpacked their shirts. Standing in front of the mirror, they dressed, Richie not bothering to take off his winter hat. Noah stared into the mirror and noticed again how the points of his collar reached his shoulders.

"Do the Descenders really hate us this much?" he asked. The teenagers who trained the scouts every week were the ones who had chosen the shirts.

Richie shrugged. "They must."

The boys gathered up their stuff and headed outside, where Megan and Ella were already waiting. They soon reached Koala Kastle. The building looked like a real castle, a tower with battlements in each corner. A fake drawbridge crossed a wimpy moat and led to a pair of glass doors, the exhibit's entrance. A nearby sign read "Closed for Construction!" Noah pulled out his special zoo key, glanced over his shoulders to ensure no one was around, then unlocked one door. Just as the scouts started to head inside, a voice rose behind him.

"You kids be careful in there."

Noah stuffed the key back into his pocket and allowed the door to ease shut. The scouts spun around and came face-to-face with Charlie Red.

"Charlie!" Megan said. "Where did you . . ."

On the drawbridge, Charlie stood perfectly still, leaves spinning around his feet and falling into the moat. His hair, as red as a cooked lobster, whipped back and forth on top of his head, and his big dark freckles stood out on his otherwise pale skin. Behind him the zoo was desolate and gray. Noah couldn't figure out how the security guard had walked up behind them so quickly.

Ella said, "Red—you are *such* a freak. You trying to give us a heart attack or something?"

"You kids be careful in there," Charlie said, echoing himself.

"Ummm . . . *weirdo* . . ." Ella spoke up. "You just said that."

There was a strange emptiness in Charlie's eyes. When he forced a smile, Noah saw how chapped and cracked and swollen his lips were.

"Charlie?" Noah said. "You okay, man?"

Charlie widened his smile a bit more, revealing yellow gunk wedged between his teeth. Something about his smile reminded Noah of a jack-o'-lantern's.

Ella said, "Red—you lose your toothbrush or something?"

Charlie only continued to stare at the scouts, his wind-tossed hair swatting his brow and curling around his ears. "I'm watching you," he uttered at last. "I see *everything* you do."

With that, he dropped his smile, scanned the scouts a final time, then turned. As he walked across the draw-bridge, the scouts watched him go. A minute later, he took a path headed toward Penguin Palace and disappeared behind a row of trees.

"Talk about a creep show," Richie said.

Ella said, "We need him getting weirder like we need Richie getting smarter."

"Forget it," Noah said. "We've got DeGraff to worry about." He abruptly turned, fitted his key back into the keyhole, and pulled on the handle.

The building consisted of an open courtyard surrounded by stone walls. Noah led the scouts down the first hall, which was lined on one side with arched windows. The friends turned to a window and looked out into the yard—a neat, grassy plain covered by a gabled glass roof. It had six sides, each a different length. The open space was crowded with eucalyptus trees, their slender leaves dangling above an assortment of stone benches, fountains, and two wells with short circular walls.

Ten koalas lived in the courtyard. With dark snouts and fuzzy Mickey Mouse–like ears, they sat nestled in the crooks of tree branches, sometimes sleeping, other times staring out at the world. A few strolled around, sniffing interesting spots on the ground and gobbling up freshly fallen eucalyptus leaves. Noah watched as one hopped onto a stone bench, stood on its hind legs, and took a sniff of the air, its black snout wriggling.

From around the corner came Solana. She was wearing her usual outfit: ripped jeans, a blue leather jacket, and fingerless gloves. She had dark eyes, high cheekbones, and long hair that trailed down her back and shoulders. Seeing her now, Noah could hardly believe she could raise quills all along her arms and torso, shooting them out through holes in her clothes. As she approached, Ella called out, "DeGraff—did you get him?"

Solana shook her head and Noah and Ella groaned, Megan banged her fists against her thighs, and Richie kicked at something on the ground.

"Man!" Ella said. "I thought for sure . . . What happened?"

"We just lost him. So did the tarsiers. He must have gone to the shadows again."

Noah held his arms out to his sides. "This is *nuts*! How are we supposed to catch someone who can do this!"

Solana kept quiet. Her silence spoke the terrifying truth: No one really knew the answer to Noah's question—not Solana, not the Descenders, not Mr. Darby or the others in the Secret Council.

"Why in the *world* was he at my house?" Ella asked.

Solana shrugged. "I wish I knew. Council's exploring the possibilities."

Everyone became quiet. After some time, Solana lifted herself onto the ledge of an open window and said, "We can't worry about it now—let's get to work." She swung her legs around and jumped down to Koala Kourtyard.

Megan was the first to follow. Noah and Ella went next, and last came Richie, the not-so-courageous scout wriggling onto the ledge, his shiny running shoes reflecting light and spotting the ornate halls of Koala Kastle. He fell into the courtyard and jumped to his feet, smiling weakly.

The scouts followed Solana beneath several eucalyptus trees, ducking their lower branches. Toward the middle of the courtyard, a few curious koalas began to trail them. Solana stopped at one of the two wells. Standing as high as her waist, its circular wall had stone blocks fitted together like the pieces of a jigsaw puzzle.

Solana placed her hand on the well. "Old castles—they

used to have these." She clapped her palm against the stone. "Take a look."

Before the scouts could reach the well, a koala did. It jumped on the ledge.

"This is Ko," Solana said. She reached out and scratched the koala's head between its near-cartoonish ears. "She's female."

When Ko sniffed Solana's fingers and suddenly jumped into the well, Richie gasped and pressed his hand over his mouth.

"I hope that thing's not as deep as a real well," Ella said. "If it is, Ko's not going to be so cuddly cute anymore."

From inside the well, Ko poked up her head and glanced around, her black snout wriggling. The scouts dashed forward and peered over the stone ledge. Ko was standing on a stone spiral staircase that wound its way into the dark depths.

"The Grottoes are just down there," Solana explained.

"But what about that one?" Richie asked, his finger aimed at the other well.

"Take a look."

The scouts jogged across the courtyard and peered into the second well. It was full of water. To Solana, Richie said, "Is this one real?"

"Nope. If we want water, we get it from the drinking fountains. That one leads to the Polar Pool, Penguin

Palace, the Wotter Park—a bunch of places."

The scouts stared into the water and considered this. Even after having trained with the Secret Society for a year, Noah still found everything amazing—all the tunnels and the wild way they connected the two zoos.

Ella reached into the well and flicked water at Richie, who stared flatly back at her, his cheeks and glasses spotted.

"Is that supposed to be funny?" Richie asked.

Smiling, Ella apologized. "Sorry—just felt like the thing to do."

From behind them, Solana said, "C'mon—let's go."

The scouts hurried back to the first well. As Noah moved in beside Solana, he noticed her again. Her leather jacket, marked with velvet patches, stopped at her narrow waist, and her faded jeans clung to her muscular legs. When Solana unexpectedly met his gaze, Noah felt embarrassed for some reason and quickly looked away.

"Who wants to go first?" Ella asked.

Megan answered by taking a seat on the ledge. She threw her legs over the wall and dropped onto the spiral staircase beside Ko. Then she took a few steps down the stairs to make room for her friends.

Ella climbed over the ledge. With some effort, Richie went next, and Noah and Solana followed. As Megan led them down the stairs, Ko jumped onto Ella's back and gripped her shoulders. Ella turned her head, a puzzled and somewhat frightened look on her face.

"Ummm . . . excuse me?" Ella said to Ko.

"She likes you," Solana said with a chuckle. "You should feel honored—she doesn't piggyback on everyone."

"It must be your ears," Richie said, referring to Ella's pink earmuffs. "They look like hers, only pink."

Ella discovered Ko's hand on her left shoulder and said, "Ummm . . . why does this thing have two thumbs?"

"All koalas do," Solana said. "It's one of the things that makes them great climbers."

As Ella followed Megan, she reached behind her and hoisted the koala by her rump into a more comfortable position, saying, "I swear . . . rip my jacket and I'll rip off your ears."

Ko simply sniffed at Ella's neck.

The stairs were steep and tough to navigate. As the scouts and Solana left behind the natural light, wall-mounted lamps began to illuminate the deep shaft.

"How deep is this thing?" Megan asked.

"I'm not sure," Solana said. "A hundred feet, maybe."

A koala charged toward them from below. He cast the group a curious glance, lamplight gleaming in his dark eyes, and hurried past. As Ko turned her head to watch her companion go, her big ear scooped up Ella's ponytail and flipped it into the air.

The cold air began to smell and taste like the earth. After a few minutes, a velvet curtain appeared in the wall, its bottom edge cut to fit the staircase. Megan stopped in front of it and looked back at Solana.

"This the one?" Megan asked. When Solana nodded, Megan added, "Anyone mind if I go first?"

Everyone answered no except Richie, who answered with his own question: "Anyone mind if I don't go at all?"

With a smile, Megan adjusted her sporty headband, took a deep breath, and stepped from the depths of the well into the Grottoes.

◅❧ CHAPTER 9 ❧▻

THE SECRET KOALA KASTLE

Noah followed his friends into a tunnel lined with the same stones that shaped the spiral staircase. Little more than five feet wide and ten feet high, it had ten branches, five on each side. A velvet curtain, each a unique color, hung at the mouth of each branch. As Noah walked, he read the metal plates above the entryways: "The Lions' Lair," "The Secret Metr-APE-olis," "The Secret Arctic Town." As he neared a tunnel marked "Little Dogs of the Prairie," four prairie dogs charged out from beneath its orange curtain, leaving its yellow tassels dancing. They weaved through the scouts, stopping at Richie's flashy shoes to give them a curious sniff.

"How's P-Dog?" Richie asked.

One prairie dog looked up and yipped.

Richie turned to Ella. "What's that supposed to mean?"

"Beats me. I don't speak prairie dog."

The prairie dogs ran circles through the Crossers' legs, then disappeared back where they'd come from.

Ella turned to Solana. "What the heck are they doing?"

Solana shrugged. "The prairie dogs are crazy."

"That explains their love for Richie."

Megan stepped through an entrance marked "The Secret Koala Kastle" and everyone followed. As the curtain dropped down Noah's back, he squirmed into a spot along his friends, who had all abruptly stopped to gaze out at the spectacle before them.

"Koala Hall," Solana said. "The core of the Secret Koala Kastle."

Koala Hall was half the size of a football field and more than forty feet high—a tremendous open space contained by stone walls and a ceiling of four stained-glass domes. More stained-glass windows were set in the walls, and the room seemed to bask in their color and patterns—ovals and diamonds and swirls of bright white light. Koalas were everywhere, resting on ledges, clinging to columns, and sleeping in eucalyptus trees, which stood all around. The koalas seemed to change color as they moved.

The Crossers stepped onto the top landing of a wide, winding stairway with rows of gold, braided balusters. Near the ground, the stairway widened, spilling onto the floor like the train of a wedding gown.

Solana headed down and the scouts followed, a plush carpet soft under their feet. At one point, the stairway split to allow a tall eucalyptus tree to pass through. As the scouts walked around the tree, Richie reached out and stripped off a piece of loose bark. He twirled it in his fingers and studiously looked it over.

"*Eucalyptus ovata,*" he said.

Ella stared at Richie, her look of confusion bordering on concern.

"Swamp gum," Richie said, as if this might explain something.

"Sounds tasty," said Ella. "Does it come in sugarless?"

As the scouts followed Solana off the stairway, Megan pointed to Ko and started laughing.

"What's so funny?" Ella asked.

"She's asleep!"

The koala had her legs drawn up against Ella's body, her arms draped over her shoulders, and her claws stuck in her poofy pink jacket.

"You're joking, right?"

Megan shook her head. "Should I get her down?"

Ella thought about this, then said, "It's no big deal. I

think my spine broke a few minutes ago anyway."

As Solana escorted them across Koala Hall, Noah stared up at the domes and thought of four supernovas, stars exploding into waves of colorful light. His falling gaze happened to land on Solana, and he realized again how pretty she was. When Solana turned her head and accidentally met his stare, Noah smiled and felt the warm rush of embarrassment in his cheeks. Solana casually winked and looked away.

Something struck his hip, knocking him sideways. Next to him was Ella, her hands propped on her hips, her eyebrows pulled down.

"What?" Noah asked. "What's the matter?" He realized he was keeping his voice low so no one else could hear.

Ella made a farting sound with her lips. "You have *got* to be kidding me!" As she walked into a new stream of reds and blues, she leaned toward him and whispered, "Was that . . . were you *flirting* with her?"

Noah cheeks began to burn. "*What?* I wasn't—"

"She's three years older than you! Not to mention she sort of lives in the ground. And she's got quills!"

Noah glanced around to make certain no one was hearing their conversation and said, "Two."

"To *what?*"

Noah held up a pair of fingers that turned green in a beam of light. "Two. She's two years older."

"Well . . . that's two too many." She pulled away and joined Megan, who was still admiring the castle.

Noah shook his head.

Their group reached the end of Koala Hall at a door marked "Koala Krossings." As Solana pulled the handle, an iron rod shaped like a eucalyptus leaf, the rusty hinges squealed and then the five of them stepped out into the open air to be greeted by a loud, powerful wind. Megan's pigtails and Ella's ponytail whipped about. Ko awoke on Ella's back. They walked onto a long wooden drawbridge. Across from them, the bridge ended at an opening in the side of a mountain, and beneath them was a deep ravine.

"The Cliff Barrier," Solana half shouted to get her voice above the sound of the wind. "It's what makes the Secret Koala Kastle a unique sector."

"Koala Kastle's surrounded by a mountain?" Noah asked.

"Mountains, actually. A range. The open areas between the mountains are closed with stone walls." Solana pointed far down the cliff. "Like that."

The scouts peered out to where a huge wall had been built between the peaks of two neighboring mountains. The top of the wall had a crenulated parapet—a walkway beside a low, protective wall.

Richie said, "I think we all know what's on the other side of the mountain—and it's *not* the bear."

Noah turned to Solana. "The City of Species?"

Solana nodded.

Built into the mountain wall were turrets—small towers with cone-shaped roofs. Noah saw dozens. Thin poles stood on their pointed peaks, holding flags shaped like eucalyptus leaves. Battlements connected all the turrets, reaching out across the rocky slope, weaving around rocks and occasional trees. On several of the protected walkways, people were pacing about. Dressed nothing like castle soldiers, they seemed out of place with their surroundings. Noah peered close and realized they were teenagers, not much older than Solana.

"Who are they?" Noah asked.

"Descenders," Solana said. "They're posted at Koala Kastle."

"How many?" Richie asked.

"Enough."

"What are they supposed to be doing?" Ella asked. "Making sure the koalas don't fall out of the trees?"

Solana shook her head. "DeGraff. We've stepped up our guard since last night."

Noah walked farther out onto the drawbridge for a better look at Koala Kastle. The castle itself wasn't all there was to this sector; he saw houses and halls of unnamable purposes. Towers rose from rocks, and arched bridges joined buildings. Fountains sprang from grassy courtyards crowded with eucalyptus trees. Flags whipped and snapped, each a flutter of unique color. Koalas were everywhere. Set in the rocky range of mountains, Koala Kastle seemed a world unto itself.

Solana and the other scouts headed over to Noah, Richie clinging to his cap and Ella her earmuffs. Still speaking against the wind, Solana said, "Four drawbridges connect Koala Kastle to the Cliff Barrier, one on each side."

Richie walked to the side of the drawbridge and stared down into the ravine. "It's a moat—we're standing above a giant moat!"

Solana nodded.

Ella asked, "What's that freaky-looking building over there?" She was pointing to a tall tower on an isolated part of the mountain. It had no walkways, and its dark windows were barred.

"It's a prison."

"A *prison*? For who—bad koalas?"

"For"—Solana seemed to search for an answer—"for others."

Noah thought this more than a bit strange. Who was the Secret Society keeping prisoner? The sasquatches? Until recently they'd all been barricaded in the Dark Lands.

"C'mon," Solana said as she brushed past the scouts. "Let's finish crossing."

The scouts followed Solana across the bridge. Above them, slender eucalyptus leaves dangled and swayed like palm fibers on a hula skirt. They passed groups of koalas which largely ignored them, their dark eyes focused on other things.

The drawbridge ended at a turret mounted to the Cliff Barrier, where a doorway was covered with a velvet curtain. Along the bottom edge of the curtain, windblown tassels brushed fallen leaves back and forth. Following Solana, Noah pushed through with one shoulder and swept the curtain across his back, feeling the magic course through his body once again.

CHAPTER 10

The City Streets

As the scouts stepped into the City of Species, the view still managed to take their breath away. Trees and buildings shared the streets. Weighty limbs punched through stone walls, and waterfalls spilled from balconies. Like a leafy canopy, branches blotted out much of the sky, their leaves flitting down in momentary streaks of autumn color. A steady breeze moved clouds of mist.

Rhinos and elephants plodded across concrete courtyards. Geckos and frogs spotted brick walls. Lemurs and tarsiers crowded the treetops. Most of the buildings housed sectors, and each had at least one doorway draped by a velvet curtain, a magical passageway to get inside. Above the curtains, colorful flags displayed sector numbers. With a glance down the street, Noah saw Sectors 4, 28, 53, and 34.

In the distance, Noah spotted the Secret Wotter Park, a sector inside a skyscraping water tower. The only way down from it was on glass slides that wound through the streets and dumped into large fountains. Noah had once ridden one of them. He'd never forget diving through the city on a rush of bubbling water, his body tunneling through treetops and hooking around the corners of buildings.

Several blocks over from the Secret Wotter Park was the octagon-shaped Library of the Secret Society, its towering walls ending at a domed glass roof. A year ago Noah had ridden Blizzard through its maze of massive bookshelves. The library was where Mr. Darby, sitting with Tank and the Descenders at Fountain Forum, had officially invited the scouts to join the Secret Society as Crossers.

An ostrich bumped into Ella and rustled its feathers, startling Ko. The big flightless bird poked forward its knotty head and hissed, prompting the koala to reach across Ella's shoulder and swat its beak, sending the ostrich off in a rush.

Ella glanced back at Ko. "You go, girl!"

Ko let down her guard and settled back into position, holding onto Ella's shoulders.

An unexpected voice rose up: "I see Ella has made a new friend."

The scouts turned to see Mr. Darby. Sunlight caught in the old man's gray hair—his ponytail, his eyebrows, the *poof* of his bushy beard. He wore dark sunglasses, and wrinkles bloomed from the hidden corners of his eyes. As usual, he was wearing a velvet trench coat, this one orange. Mr. Darby's normal playful manner was nowhere to be found. His face was tight with tension—no doubt because of DeGraff.

Beside Mr. Darby was Tank, the biggest, toughest, and one of the kindest men Noah had ever known. Standing close to seven feet, his entire body was a collection of muscles; they bulged like bendable balloons tied in knots. He had dark skin and a shiny bald head and stood with his arms crossed and the corners of his lips curled down. Like Mr. Darby, he was strictly business today.

Around the two of them were some of the animals assigned to the scouts' crosstraining. Blizzard, a mighty polar bear with a back long and strong enough to simultaneously carry all the scouts. Little Bighorn, a rhinoceros with a bad temper and a knack for barreling through walls. Podgy, an emperor penguin who'd learned to fly. And Marlo, a thumb-size malachite kingfisher assigned to carry messages between the scouts and a few people in the Secret Zoo.

Blizzard nudged Noah with his heavy snout, nearly knocking him over. Marlo touched down on his shoulder and chirped. Ko leaned over and sniffed curiously at Little Bighorn.

To Solana, Mr. Darby asked, "How much time until the scouts must find their way home?"

"About a half hour, I guess."

"Good," Mr. Darby said. "Then please follow me. We need a comfortable place to discuss some things." He turned and started walking, his long trench coat dragging colorful leaves across the street.

"Uh-oh," Ella said as she hoisted Ko up on her back. "When you start talking about comfortable places to talk, it usually means you have something *un*comfortable to say."

"Indeed I do," Mr. Darby said. "Indeed I do."

✿ CHAPTER 11 ✿

THE SPECTERS

The scouts followed Mr. Darby past a tall brick building with a banner reading "Sector 98—Platypus Playground" to an open-walled wooden hut. Beneath a thatched roof were three circles of pillowy chairs, and Mr. Darby, with a sweep of his arm, invited the scouts to sit down. As Ella took a seat beside Richie, Ko jumped to the wide back of her chair, cradling it like a limb of a eucalyptus tree.

Noah watched a group of platypuses enter the City of Species from Platypus Playground. They had streamlined bodies and strange, rubbery bills that reminded Noah of giant shoehorns. One stepped into the hut, dragging its beaverlike tail and slapping the ground with its webbed feet.

Richie's flashy running shoes caught the interest of the odd animal, which wandered over and sniffed at them, its bill swinging like a pinball flipper. When the platypus lifted its front feet up onto Richie's shins, Richie flinched and pulled back, burying the greater part of his torso in the deep cushions of the chair.

Solana said, "He wants you to pet him."

Richie eyes were wide, his lips pinched tight. "With . . . with my *hand*?"

"No . . ." Ella said. "With your *butt*."

Richie slowly reached out. He touched the platypus's head with two fingers and quickly pulled his arm back.

"There," he said to the platypus while wiping his hand on his zoo uniform. "Now, go away. Shoo."

The platypus jumped down and hurried off, both ends of its body—its bill and its tail—swinging in a similar way.

Everyone else took a seat except for Tank, who stood behind Mr. Darby and Solana, his beefy arms crossed over his beefy chest. Next to Richie was an empty chair, but when Richie motioned for Tank to sit in it, the big man waved off the invitation. Mr. Darby adjusted his sunglasses, cleared his throat with an attention-getting rumble, and turned to Ella.

"DeGraff," he said as he leaned forward in his chair. "Tell me what happened."

Ella recounted the story—the tap on her window, DeGraff standing in her front yard, the prairie dogs jumping onto him, and finally his escape. Mr. Darby didn't interrupt once. At one point a frown found his face; at another he began to rub his temples. When Ella was done talking, he turned to Tank and the two communicated something serious with their eyes.

"He's coming for us," Mr. Darby said at last. "For the first time since we drove him out of the Secret Zoo—the Shadowist is coming."

The idea forced everyone into silence. The only sounds came from the animal traffic along the city streets—grunts and hisses and clomping hooves. Just outside the hut, leaves continue to fall from the heights like rain.

"Can we stop him?" Noah heard himself say. He'd never meant to speak—the words seemed to push out of him.

Mr. Darby rubbed the back of his neck in a worried way. "We have prepared for this for more than eighty years—our Crossers, our Descenders, our perimeter patrols. We knew this day might come, and we are ready. But . . ." The old man's voice trailed off. He seemed to lack the courage to say more.

"But what?" Noah asked.

Mr. Darby kept quiet. He combed his fingers through

his bushy beard and then stroked some wrinkles out of his velvet jacket. Finally, he said, "DeGraff is a man . . . a *half* man . . . a *creature* that can drift in and out of the shadows. As he gets closer to the zoo, his magic only grows." He stopped, glanced at Tank, then turned his head to stare out at the City of Species. "How do we stop a thing like that?"

"You capture him!" Noah spat out. "We get to him before he can get to the shadows."

"The shadows are everywhere."

"But DeGraff can only use his magic in the deepest ones. We just need to grab him while he's still in the light. The moonlight—that's enough light, right?"

Mr. Darby continued to stare out at his beloved city in a contemplative way. "There is much we don't know." His voice was quiet, reserved. All of his usual animation was gone, and Noah hated the way he looked so defeated.

Megan spoke next: "Then we step up our efforts!"

Mr. Darby turned back to the group and forced his frown flat. "Exactly what we intend to do." He paused for a few seconds, then went on. "Because you're members of our Secret Society—and especially because you live in the neighborhood around the Clarksville Zoo—I feel you have a right to know something." He leaned toward the four friends and announced, "We're sending more Descenders into the outside world."

Everyone became quiet again. Then Noah turned back to Mr. Darby and said, "But how? You can't have a bunch of teenagers guarding the zoo all night!"

"You can if no one sees them."

The scouts traded confused looks.

"Mr. Darby," Ella said. "You guys might be able to hide tarsiers in the trees, but hiding one of these guys"—Ella pointed to Solana—"is *not* going to be so easy."

A smile found the old man's lips. "No? Then, please . . . tell me how many Descenders you see. In this hut, right now, with us."

The scouts looked around.

"One," Noah said. "Solana."

"You're certain?"

The scouts glanced around again. Ella stared at the rafters, and Richie peered beneath his chair.

"Just Solana," Noah repeated.

Mr. Darby turned to Tank, and the two men smiled.

Tank said, "Looks like it's going to work, Mr. D."

The scouts just sat there, confused.

After a few seconds, Ella said, "Uhhh . . . you guys have peanut butter and crazy sandwiches for lunch?"

"Look more closely," Mr. Darby said. "At the chairs. Look at the one beside Richie. Don't see what's there—see what *isn't* there."

Noah looked at the empty chair next to his friend. It

had a high, arched back and bulged with thick padding. The fabric had swirling designs.

Noah said, "Mr. Darby . . . what are you getting at? I don't see anything."

"That's precisely the point."

Noah squinted toward the chair. Again he saw the height of its back, the rounded swell of the armrests, the—

His thoughts stopped. A depression in the seat cushion had just shifted.

See what isn't there, Mr. Darby had said.

He realized something. The air above the seat was moving, as if a faint fog hovered just above the cushions. Then the movement stopped.

"Did you see?" Mr. Darby said.

Still squinting, Noah said, "I saw . . . *something.*"

"See it again."

Richie was looking between Noah and the empty chair beside him. "Uhhh . . . what are you guys talking about?" He nervously leaned toward Ella. From the high back of Ella's chair, Ko poked her snout toward Richie and sniffed the jittery pom-pom on his hat.

"I'm with Richie this time," Ella said. "You two are *totally* freaking me out."

Noah paid little mind to his friends. He kept focused on the chair—the space above its seat cushion. He saw nothing for a few seconds. Then, halfway up the back of the chair, something in the air made the colors and patterns in the cushion's fabric move.

"Did you see?" Mr. Darby asked.

Noah didn't move his eyes. "Yes."

Now everyone was staring intensely at the space, even Ko. They were watching and waiting.

Seconds passed. New movement appeared at the base of the chair, almost at the ground.

"I saw it," Megan said.

"Me, too," said Ella.

"Saw what?" asked Richie. He was leaning so far away from the mysterious chair that he was almost horizontal, his head nearly on Ella's legs.

Another whirl of movement, this time at the forward edge of the seat cushion, in the place someone's knees would be. As quickly as it came, it left.

"Saw it," Noah said.

"Keep watching," instructed Mr. Darby.

Something appeared along the high back of the chair. A speck of white. What first looked like a small ball revealed itself as something else. An eye. A human eye surrounded by a patch of light skin. Seeming to hover in space, the eye was staring back at everyone else.

Richie yelped and flipped over his armrest, landing in Ella's lap before rolling to the floor.

The eye blinked once, twice. Then it was gone again. Noah watched as the seat cushions swelled back to their normal shape. It was as if someone had risen out of the chair.

In front of the chair, the air moved. Then again, this time farther away. And again, farther still. It was certain, now—something had risen out of the seat and was advancing toward Mr. Darby and Tank.

"What is it?" Megan asked.

New spots of movement suddenly began to appear above and below one another. The areas expanded and joined, and the once-shapeless thing began to take form. Arms, legs, torso. A ghostly human that Noah could see clear through.

"Come meet the scouts," Mr. Darby said to the thing taking shape.

A small piece of the developing figure broke free and fell to the ground. Then another piece, and another. As the fragments hit the floor, they came into view, filling with color and contour. Noah could barely believe his eyes. Chameleons. They skittered across the wooden planks.

"No way," Megan gasped.

More and more chameleons began to rain down. They had beady eyes and knobby heads. A few had horns. And they were all colors: green with blue stripes, teal with brown dots, even full rainbows in speckled patterns. They fell like chunks of snow from a melting snowman. The details of the person began to appear: the fair skin of a hand, the shoulder of a white shirt, a green pants leg.

By the time at least twenty chameleons had dropped to the ground, a young teenage girl was revealed. She wore camouflage cargo pants covered in pouches and pockets, a few with velvet patches. She had on black hiking boots with bright yellow stripes, and a pullover sweatshirt with a deep hood. The sides of her hair were clipped to dramatically different lengths, and her bangs fell at an angle down to her chin, concealing most of her face. She had her hands on her hips, her elbows out. The chameleons lay at her feet, a spill of spectacular color on the dull brown wood.

"Scouts, meet Evie," Mr. Darby casually said.

Evie nodded at the scouts, who were too stunned to move.

"And the others?" Mr. Darby said.

Evie tipped up her chin and said, "Come out, girls."

In different places, the air began to move. The swirling spots quickly took on human shapes as chameleons rained down. Within seconds five young teenage girls were revealed—two sitting on the wooden rail, two perched on the arms of the chairs in the nearby circle, and one standing next to Tank. They were similarly dressed in hooded shirts and cargo pants with big pockets and velvet patches.

For what seemed a long time, no one said a word. It was Mr. Darby who finally broke the silence: "My dear scouts, I'd like you to meet our friends the Specters."

"'Specters,'" Richie said, repeating the word. Then he translated it into something new: *"Ghosts."*

"They've been here all along?" Ella asked. "Since we came into the hut?"

"Heavens, no!" Mr. Darby answered. "They've been following you since *long* before then. Since Koala Kourtyard—am I correct, Solana?"

The Descender nodded.

From his spot on the ground, Richie asked, "Am I the only one finding that a bit creepy?"

Ella stood up, grabbed Richie's shirt, and yanked him to his feet. "Seriously?" she said, as if suddenly embarrassed by her friend. She straightened Richie's gigantic collar and gently shoved him into his seat, where the air trapped in the big cushions gushed out with a loud farting sound. To Evie, Ella said, "Nice trick. You mind telling us how it works?"

Evie glanced at Mr. Darby. She opened her mouth and then closed it.

"It's okay," Mr. Darby said. "They're one of us. They've been Crossers for a year—they have a right to know."

Evie stared at Ella from behind her angled bangs. She touched a velvet patch on her pants pocket, started to say something, and then stopped. "You tell them," she said at last.

Mr. Darby said, "The chameleons do what chameleons do. But like most things in the Secret Zoo, on a far grander scale."

The old man reached down, swept up a bright green chameleon, and raised it to his face. With a fingertip, he delicately stroked the small lizard's back, saying, "Chameleons have transparent skin. Beneath their skin, they have special cells called chromatophores. These cells have a pigment that allows the chameleons to create color." Mr. Darby took a few steps forward, lowered his hand, and dropped the chameleon into a large pocket in the side of Evie's cargo pants. "Some of the Specters' pockets are lined with velvet. Magic flows from the velvet into the chameleons, modifying their chromatophores, permitting them to take on colors and tones in a very sophisticated way."

The chameleon escaped from Evie's pocket and crawled up her leg. As it went, small pieces of Evie seemed to vanish. The chameleon made its way to her shoulder and stopped, leaving a wake of apparent invisibility across her torso and leg—it looked as if a long, two-inch strip of the girl had somehow been removed.

"The chameleons spread out across the Specters, blending them into their surroundings. This act of camouflage is controlled by their chameleons' thoughts—they control the process."

Having spent a year crosstraining in the Secret Zoo, Noah had seen the impossible made possible too many times to count. This was no exception.

"Does it . . . hurt?" Megan asked.

"Nothing hurts," Evie injected into the conversation. "Not for long."

Mr. Darby smiled and said, "I am told it *tingles*."

"So the girls just walk around all day covered in lizards?" Ella said. "That's got to make it pretty tough on the social life—not to mention taking a pee."

"The chameleons only come out when they're needed."

"But where do they come from?" Noah asked. He again noticed the velvet patches on the big pockets in the Specters' pants. "I have a feeling those pockets aren't normal."

Mr. Darby smiled. "You're right about that. The chameleons portal into their pockets the same way we portal into the Secret Zoo's many sectors. In Streets of Transparency, the chameleon sector in the Secret Zoo, there's a special area called the Portal Place. It's used only by the Specters. Each pocket opens to the Portal Place, and chameleons portal when they're needed by the

Specters. But you've seen this magic before."

Ella said, "Yeah, but we've never seen animals jumping in and out of peoples' pants. That's a big-time new trick."

Noah turned to the chameleons. They blanketed a good part of the floor and clung to the chairs and perimeter railing, saturating the hut with bright oranges, purples, reds, and blues. Their bulbous eyes rolled in their sockets, each staring off in its own direction.

Mr. Darby turned to Tank and said, "Mr. Pangbourne— would you care to formally introduce the Specters?"

"Sure thing, Mr. D." As the big man plodded into the middle of the circle, the chameleons scattered away from his massive feet. He clapped Evie on the shoulder and said, "As you know, this is Evie. She sort of leads the pack."

Evie nodded toward the scouts.

Tank gestured to the two girls sitting on chairs in the neighboring circle. "Over there are Kaleena and Jordynn."

Kaleena had long hair set in dozens of braids that fell from an uneven part down the center of her head; high, round cheekbones; and deep brown skin. She wore camouflage pants and a black sweatshirt. Jordynn had an Afro that stood at least six inches off her head, a pair of green cargo pants, blue hiking shoes, and a yellow sweatshirt.

Tank motioned to the two girls seated on the railing and said, "That's Elakshi and Lee-Lee."

Elakshi had lustrous hair that trailed down her back and shoulders. Her eyes were nearly as dark as her coal-black hair. She wore a pair of white camouflage pants, black boots, and a black hoodie. Lee-Lee had long bangs that parted to one side. Her straight, collar-length hair curved inward to a point just below her chin, covering her ears and the sides of her face. Her plump lips were set in a smirk. She wore dark green pants and a thin hooded sweatshirt that clung to her arms and waist.

Tank gestured to where he'd been standing behind Mr. Darby. "And back there's Sara."

Sara had a punk look. The top of her blond hair was combed to a Mohawk, and long bangs fell to one side of her face just above her chin. She wore black eye shadow, glossy lipstick, and strips of pink blush. Like her friends, she was dressed in camouflage pants and a hooded shirt. She also had a green bandana tied around her arm.

Tank turned back to the scouts. "The Specters. That's all of them."

Ella said, "You sure there's not like a hundred more creeping around? Or how about in the Clarksville Zoo? They could be tiptoeing through our neighborhood!"

Mr. Darby stepped toward the scouts, the chameleons scattering at his feet, and raised one eyebrow above his sunglasses. "Not yet."

"Uh-oh . . ." Richie said. "What are you guys planning?"

The old man came out with it: "Operation Divide and Descend. An action against DeGraff. An aggressive assault which involves posting the Specters in your very own yards."

CHAPTER 12

OPERATION DIVIDE AND DESCEND

"Let's hear it," Noah said.

Mr. Darby said, "In addition to our normal activities, we'll send the Specters into your neighborhood—at dusk, when the shadows are fullest and DeGraff is most likely to move. We'll divide them around the border of the Clarksville Zoo. Unlike the tarsiers, who need to hide in the trees, the Specters will be able to move along the ground. If one spots DeGraff, she'll alert the Descenders. And together, they'll do what the Descenders do best. Descend—descend with their full power."

"Their *gear*?" Richie asked, referring to the magical

equipment that gave the teenagers their incredible animal skills.

Mr. Darby nodded.

Megan said, "But . . . right in our *neighborhood*! What if someone sees?"

It was Solana who answered. "The streetlights in your neighborhood—they're sparse. And there are plenty of places to hide. If a chase happens, we'll keep to the darkness. As much as we can, anyway."

"I don't like this," Noah said. "The risk is so—"

"But what do you suppose we risk by not stopping DeGraff?" Mr. Darby interrupted. "Which risk do you suppose is greater?"

No one said a thing.

"I assure you, there is no other way. We must move to the offensive if DeGraff is to be defeated."

Megan asked, "How will the Specters contact the Descenders?"

Mr. Darby nodded at Solana, who stepped forward and pulled something out of her pocket—a headset, the tiny earphones the Descenders wore. She reached toward Evie, the headset in her open palm.

Evie stared down at the headset, seemed to consider something, then turned away. Solana shared a disappointed look with Mr. Darby, then stuffed the equipment back into her pocket, saying to Evie, "Well . . . you know where to get one if you change your mind."

The scouts passed a confused look among themselves.

"The Specters will flag the tarsiers," Mr. Darby answered. "The ones on patrol. The tarsiers will then alert the owls, as they normally would."

Ella asked the obvious: "But why not the headsets?"

Mr. Darby glanced at Evie, then Solana. After a few seconds, he simply said, "They'll use the tarsiers."

Noah couldn't figure out why Evie seemed so reluctant to talk. And why did it seem that she didn't like Solana? He turned to the other Specters. They seemed emotionless. He noticed the way they looked again—Kaleena's hair a cascade of heavy braids, Jordynn's a tuft of weightless curls. On the railing Lee-Lee sat dangling her legs, and Elakshi leaned coolly against a beam. Sara stood with her hip cocked out, her blue eyes buried in black smudges of makeup. The Specters. Six peculiar girls who could vanish in the camouflage of chameleons. Six ghosts.

✿ CHAPTER 13 ✿

WIDE WALT STRIKES

At afternoon recess two days later, the scouts headed out to the playground among a swell of crazed kids. Noah ducked under a swinging bridge, Megan swung around a set of monkey bars, Ella dodged a second grader flying off a slide, Richie nearly got flattened by a fourth grader taking a flying leap off a climbing wall, and they all met up by the soccer field for a private spot to discuss the Specters again. Just a few minutes into their conversation, Marlo flew in and touched down on Noah's shoulder. The scouts were barely startled—the kingfisher was so tiny that he could drop in almost anytime and not risk being spotted.

He had a folded-up piece of paper pinched in his bill.

"Hey, Marlo," Noah said as he plucked the note from the bird's pointed mouth.

Marlo chirped a greeting.

Noah unfolded the message to find two pages. The scouts gathered close and read the first, a flier from the Clarksville Zoo.

Volunteer Appreciation Night!!

This Friday and Saturday the Clarksville Zoo will be hosting its 15th Annual Volunteer Appreciation Night to honor the hard work of our generous volunteers! Because we enjoyed such a ZOOmungous number of helpers this year, the event will be hosted across two nights. The volunteers have been divided into two groups, the Lions and the Lambs. The Clarksville Zoo will host the Lions on Friday and the Lambs on Saturday. Festivities will include:

- Games at Creepy Critters!
- Dinner at Koala Kastle!
- A movie at Metr-APE-olis!
- A sleepover at the Forest of Flight!
- Breakfast at Butterfly Nets!

◡ ◡ ◡

As always, the event will be chaperoned by adult volunteers. Parental permission is mandatory for kids under seventeen! (See form below.) Anyone planning to stay the night should bring a sleeping bag and a pillow.

GET READY TO GET WILD!!!

Noah swapped the pages, and the scouts read the second note in silence. Marlo peered over Noah's shoulder, as if reading along.

Dear Scouts,

As you may know, Volunteer Appreciation Night is an annual event. This year we've divided the volunteers into groups and plan to host the event over two nights. One group will include the real volunteers, and the second group will include the four of you.

Hope to see you on Saturday night at 8:00! If you have issues with your parents or are unable to attend, please send a note back with Marlo later in the week. Otherwise, I look forward to seeing you then.

Come prepared for the competition of your life.

Sincerely,
Mr. Darby

P.S. The flier is intended to show your parents—no need to return!

"Competition?" Ella said. "What's he talking about?"

"Crosstraining," Richie said. "Our party—it's really a crosstraining session."

Noah nodded. "An all-nighter. You guys think your parents will be cool with that?"

Richie said, "My mom will think it's the neatest thing in the world!"

Ella nodded. "My mom, too."

Noah turned to Megan. "And what about Mom and Dad?"

"They'll go for it, I think."

"Okay," Noah said. "Then I'll just sign this right now."

Ella reached across Richie's lap, plucked a pen from his pocket of nerd-gear, and tossed it to Noah, who uncapped it and scribbled, "We'll see you on Saturday" onto Mr. Darby's note. Then he folded the paper and held it out for Marlo, who pecked it from his fingertips, sprang off Noah's shoulder, and shot across the playground.

"An all-nighter," Ella said.

"Oh boy," Richie said. "What are we up against now?"

The school bell ended recess. The scouts jumped to their feet and headed inside.

For Ella, the rest of the day dragged along. With all the things happening with DeGraff and the Secret Zoo, it was becoming next to impossible to concentrate on school. What did world history matter when you feared the world was about to *become* history?

v v v

At the sound of the final school bell, more than four hundred kids jumped to their feet and flooded out of their classrooms. Outside, Noah and Megan piled into their mother's car for dentist appointments, and Ella and Richie began their walk home, cutting across the playground toward Jenkins Street.

As Ella and Richie neared the end of the schoolyard, three kids appeared from out of a wooded area and approached them—Wide Walt and his two friends, Dave and Doug. Ella glanced over her shoulders to see that no one was around. This meant one thing—trouble.

"Be cool," Ella said to Richie from the corner of her mouth.

"Check this out!" Walt said as he stepped up. "Two of my favorite *dorks*!"

Walt's head looked smaller than ever against the padded shoulders of his poofy jacket. He smiled from ear to ear, displaying his lopsided teeth.

Ella said, "What do you want, Walt?"

Walt laced his fingers and pushed his arms forward, loudly cracking his knuckles. This was one of his signature moves, and it was meant to intimidate. Richie flinched.

"I want what's in your backpack."

"Huh?"

"Your backpack. I want whatever the heck's inside it—the thing that did *this* to me." He held out his hand inches from Ella's face. His index finger was badly bruised and wrapped in a Band-Aid with the picture of a Transformer.

"Megatron," Ella said. *"Niiiccce."*

Walt pulled back his hand and coiled it into a fist.

With unmoving lips, Richie whispered, "Don't . . . upset . . . him."

"You think you're funny?" Walt spat out.

"Richie's the funny one," Ella said. "Richie—why don't you tell Walt a joke?"

Richie didn't move.

Walt held out his arm. "The backpack."

"No chance, White."

"The backpack. Or we drop"—he nodded at Richie—"the nerd."

Doug took a step forward and shot out his chest a bit. He wore a white baseball cap, its flat bill cocked to one side. Beneath it, a messy mop of collar-length hair curled out, covering his ears, his neck, his forehead. He had an upturned nose that was nearly piglike. To her friends, Ella called him "the oinker."

Ella didn't know how long she could stand her ground. But if she showed weakness, the scouts would pay for it the rest of their time at Clarksville Elementary. Walt *fed* off weakness.

Ella glanced over her shoulders. Still, no one was in sight.

"You guys had this coming," Walt declared. "You got no one to blame but yourselves."

Walt nodded to Doug, who immediately sprang his arm forward, punching Richie's stomach. Air gushed from Richie and he buckled forward, his glasses shooting off his face and landing in a patch of oversized weeds. He dropped to the ground and rolled around, his eyes and mouth pinched shut.

Walt reached out and fist-tapped Doug. With his head bobbing in satisfaction—as if to a musical beat that only he could hear—he uttered his tagline: "That's what I thought."

Rage tore through Ella. Her cheeks flushed and her heart began to slam in her chest. She dove forward, reaching for Walt, who grabbed her arms and easily threw her to the ground. Dirt filled her mouth. She felt a tug on her shoulders and realized someone was stripping the pack off her back. She was yanked and bounced around. Her jaw struck the hard earth and stars began to shoot across her vision. Finally, the backpack slipped off.

She rolled over. Walt had opened her backpack and was rifling through her stuff, throwing anything that didn't interest him into the air—her books, her little purse, papers, the leftovers of her lunch. Doug and Dave cast around nervous glances—this was serious and they knew it. Not only had Walt just assaulted a girl, but he was now going through her belongings.

Ella started to say something and stopped. Not because she couldn't speak, but because she worried that she might start crying. And she wouldn't give Wide Walt the satisfaction of that.

Walt tossed out a handheld mirror given to Ella by her grandmother, then tipped over the open bag and shook out the remaining loose items—a piece of gum, a quarter, some lip balm. He threw the empty backpack aside. There was nothing in it that interested him.

Walt looked at his friends. "Whatever she had . . . it's not there anymore."

Ella's lips trembled. She was close to tears.

Walt stared down and shook his head. "I hope you turds learned something today." To his friends he said, "C'mon—let's get out of here." The three of them turned and ran. Within seconds they were gone.

Ella lay on the ground, her lips quivering. After some time, she crawled over to Richie. Her friend was still clutching his stomach. She touched his head, saying, "Your glasses . . ." She swept them out of the weeds and carefully placed them back on. She was sickened to see that one lens had a crack in it. "We're okay, Richie," she said. "They're gone now."

She noticed her belongings scattered about like litter. She climbed to her feet, claimed her backpack, and picked up a schoolbook. Then she went to her next thing, then the next, and the next. Her eyes welled with tears that blurred her vision. She turned her head to hide her face.

"We're okay," she reminded Richie as she swept up her mirror. A web of cracks ran through the glass, and a jagged piece had fallen out. "It's—"

She felt her voice shudder and swallowed back her breath. She wouldn't cry—not in front of Richie. All her friends thought of her as the strong one, the tough one. She couldn't let them down, not with so much at stake.

Memories unexpectedly filled her. She pictured DeGraff staring out at her from the shadows in her front yard as she stood all alone on her porch, no one nearby to help. She thought about her home—how different it was now, how lonely it sometimes felt, even with her mother by her side. Finally, she remembered her father, how the world had taken him away, and it was too much for Ella to bear. She turned away from Richie and allowed her tears to come.

✖ CHAPTER 14 ✖

FROM PIZZOORIA TO ZOOASIS

Noah and Megan boiled with fury when Ella and Richie told them what had happened with Walt. He'd never actually hit one of the scouts before. Their first thought was to go to an adult, but then they feared this might only make matters worse. After a long, heated discussion in Fort Scout (one in which Noah tirelessly paced back and forth and knocked over a chair in frustration), they decided to wait it out and see what might happen with Walt back at school after the weekend.

The four of them had no problems getting permission to attend the supposed volunteer party, and at dusk on

Saturday, they loaded up their packs, grabbed their sleeping bags, and headed for the Clarksville Zoo, excited but nervous about what they might find. As they pushed through the turnstiles at the front gates, the guard told them to report to PizZOOria, the big cafeteria. Across the zoo grounds, tall light posts carved cone-shaped wedges out of the darkness.

At PizZOOria they pushed through the unlocked doors to find Tank sitting at one of the cafeteria's many long benches, his fist buried in a tub of popcorn. On the tabletop beside him was a tiny, bright blue bird—Marlo. The kingfisher was pecking at a pile of popcorn Tank had given him. Behind Tank was a portable whiteboard. As the scouts dropped their stuff and approached the bench, Tank shoved a fistful of popcorn into his smile.

"Hungry?" Ella asked.

As Tank munched, he said, "When you're as big as me, you're *always* hungry."

"Makes sense. But how do you explain this?" She jerked her thumb toward Richie, who was greedily reaching for some popcorn. "This guy weighs less than his own clothes."

Tank laughed and offered the tub to Richie, who plunged his hand into it.

"He burns all his calories worrying about stuff," Tank said with a wink toward Richie.

Megan said, "Okay . . . what's on the agenda tonight?"

"Some training—an emergency session, I guess you could call it, because of the DeGraff sighting. And we're going to follow it with a test."

"Great," Ella said. "Like we don't get enough of those in school."

"It's more of a challenge—and don't worry, it's not going to kill you. At least it shouldn't, anyway." Richie's eyes widened as Tank rose from the bench. "But that's not until later. Right now, I got a whole bunch of things to review—Mr. D wants to make sure you're up to snuff. With DeGraff on the loose, we can't afford mistakes. So take a seat. And here"—he slid the tub of popcorn across the table—"help yourselves."

The big man went to the whiteboard, grabbed a marker, and for the next three hours, the five of them reviewed the Grottoes, the tunnel system beneath the Clarksville Zoo. Tank had them repeatedly come up to the whiteboard to draw pictures of particular sections. He wanted to be certain they'd memorized the passages—how they interconnected and led to different areas.

Around 11:00, Tank set down the marker, announced it was time, and donned his jacket, which was so thickly padded that it made him look a bit like a small cloud. After the scouts dressed, Marlo sprang to his usual spot on Noah's shoulder and the group stepped outside and walked to ZOOasis, a big outdoor garden surrounded by a wide web of concrete paths. Flamingo Fountain sat at its core. Mostly devoid of flowers this time of year, the garden was still alive with evergreen bushes and trees. Marble benches were scattered along the grassy paths, and when the group reached ZOOasis, they saw Mr. Darby sitting on one.

"Welcome!" Mr. Darby said as the scouts approached. Noah found it strange that the old man was wearing his sunglasses in the dark. "The four of you have come prepared for a physical challenge, yes?"

A bit unsure, the scouts nodded anyway.

"Excellent." The old man peered beyond the four children and said, "All of you, if you'll come out, please."

From around a group of shadowy bushes, the Descenders appeared—Tameron, Solana, Sam, and Hannah. They were wearing the clothes that carried their powers: leather jackets, hats, boots, and gloves. Tameron had his enormous backpack slung over his shoulders. As they neared the scouts, Sam peered out from beneath his long bangs; Tameron, from under the tilted brim of his cap. Hannah worked her jaw over her chewing gum, and Solana stood with her hands on her hips.

Ella said, "Looks like our opponents just arrived."

Hannah loudly popped her gum and winked at Ella.

Richie said, "So we're facing off against teenagers who

can fly, throw quills, smash out walls, and leap tall buildings in a single bound."

Mr. Darby turned to Tank. "Richie has a point, Mr. Pangbourne. Should we award our scouts something to compensate for the Descenders' remarkable skills?"

"Seems fair enough."

"Very well. Your animal friends—Blizzard, Podgy, Little Bighorn, any that you know personally—they may assist you." Mr. Darby turned to the kingfisher sitting on Noah's shoulder. "Marlo, will you please make sure the scouts' companions know of this?"

Marlo chirped, sprang into the air, and dashed out of sight.

"Now then . . ." Mr. Darby looked toward Tank. "Can you please explain our challenge, Mr. Pangbourne?"

"You guys ever hear of a game called Capture the Flag?" Tank asked.

The scouts nodded. They'd played Capture the Flag countless times.

"Well, this is the flag. . . ." Tank slipped a small piece of velvet from his jacket and tossed it toward the scouts. Noah snagged it. It was so thin that it was practically threadbare. "All you need to do is capture it," Tank finished.

Noah said, "It tingles."

"Unspent magic. It used to be part of a curtain." He

held out his open palm. "I'll take that back now."

As Noah handed the flag over, Mr. Darby said, "The game is a way for us to see how you compare to the Descenders—how far you've come as Crossers over the past year. With the sighting of DeGraff, the Secret Society is evaluating all its defenses."

"Where does the game take place?" Noah asked.

"Wherever the flag goes. Here probably. And in the Secret Zoo."

"But what if someone sees us running around?"

Mr. Darby said, "They won't if you keep to the shadows."

"Speaking of the shadows," Richie said. "Who's on patrol?"

"Substitutes. And of course the Specters are helping now as well."

"The rules are simple," Tank said, bringing the conversation back. "Get the flag and bring it to ZOOasis. Return it . . ." His gaze stopped on a large marble vase at the edge of a flowerbed. He hoisted it, dumped its soil, and set it in the middle of the path. "Right here," he finished. "You can steal the flag from your opponent at any point. And any use of the Grottoes or the gateways is fair game. Same with the animals—leverage them if you can. And know that most of our furry fellows are going to be trying to keep the flag away from all eight of you guys."

"Huh?" Noah said. "Why?"

Tank ignored the question and, to the scouts, said, "Remember all the things we just talked about in PizZOOria—the Grottoes and the ways they connect the zoos. Remember the shortcuts."

Noah tried to ask another question, but Tank tossed the flag into the air and yelled, "Go!"

A chickadee swooped down, snatched the flag, and flew toward Metr-APE-olis. The Descenders immediately ran across the grass after it, disappearing behind a row of bushes.

The scouts simply stood there, a bit shocked.

"Usually the flag doesn't come to you," Tank pointed out.

The four friends traded nervous glances and then took off. Just like that, the game was on.

CHAPTER 15

GAME ON

The scouts squeezed through a hedge and dodged a concession stand. At least fifty yards divided them from the Descenders. As the teenagers turned a corner of Metr-APE-olis, the scouts lost sight of them.

"We'll never catch these guys!" Richie said.

"We don't need to catch them!" said Ella. "We just need to get the flag!"

The scouts rounded Metr-APE-olis just in time to see the chickadee drop the flag over Little Dogs of the Prairie. Before it could hit the hillside, a prairie dog jumped to its haunches, chomped into it, then dove into a tunnel and disappeared.

"Did you see that?" Ella said.

"That's what Tank was talking about," said Megan. "The animals . . . they're trying to keep the flag away from us."

The Descenders rushed down the stairs leading to the concrete tunnels that ran beneath the sandy hillside. Set into the tunnels were clear, plastic domes that let kids stand up and gaze out across the exhibit. As the Descenders' heads poked up, the prairie dogs quickly piled across one another on the clear caps. Once enough weight covered a dome, it began to turn, slowly at first, then more and more rapidly, flinging prairie dogs across the plain. Within seconds, all the domes stopped, their empty spaces revealing how the Descenders had disappeared into the Grottoes the same way Ella and Richie had when they first discovered the Secret Zoo.

"C'mon!" Noah said as they reached the exhibit. "Let's go!"

He led his friends to the bottom of the steps, where they crawled into different tunnels, as the Descenders had done. Noah rose, his head partly filling the dome above him. Across the hillside, he watched the other scouts' heads rise above ground like giant gophers'. The prairie dogs immediately went to work, piling onto the domes. Within seconds, the clear cap around Noah's head dropped a few inches with a loud click, and his floor began to turn. It gained more and more speed, and then dropped several feet into the dark earth. When it stopped, Noah crawled into a new tunnel, and the platform he'd been on sprang back into the air, sealing the hole above. The other scouts soon joined him.

"Let's go!" Ella said.

They crawled in a line down the dimly lit passage. The tunnel, filled with prairie dogs, branched off in dozens of directions. At the end of the main passage, a swaying velvet curtain revealed the direction the Descenders had gone.

"They're headed to Little Dogs of the Secret Prairie!" Noah said. "And that's where the flag's going! C'mon!"

"Wait!" Megan said. "Let's split up! Ella and I—we'll take a different sector and try to head off the flag at the City of Species!"

Noah nodded. "You're going to have to be quick." He scanned the plates above the tunnels with velvet curtains and read off the names: "The Secret Ostrich Island," "The Secret Kangaroo Kampground," "The Secret Elephant Event." "Take Kangaroo Kampground," he advised. "You can use the tents to quickly portal across the sector. Plus it opens in the City of Species right beside Little Dogs of the Secret Prairie."

"Good idea," Ella said. "You'd make Tank proud." The

girls crawled into the Secret Kangaroo Kampground and were gone.

Noah said, "Richie—we've got to hurry!"

Together, the boys rushed forward and chased after the Descenders into the Secret Zoo.

CHAPTER 16

LITTLE DOGS OF THE SECRET PRAIRIE

Noah and Richie stepped into Little Dogs of the Secret Prairie and were met with a blast of hot air and blinding light. A dusty grassland reached out in all directions, patches of tall grass and cacti rising from the landscape. The hard ground was pitted with countless holes that hundreds of prairie dogs dove in and out of. Far across the sector, a colorful light blinked on and off—the entrance into the City of Species. About fifty yards from the cave, the Descenders chased the prairie dog with the flag. The teenagers hadn't geared up, which meant the scouts still had a chance.

"There they are!" Noah called out. "Let's go!"

The two boys raced forward, their feet sweeping up clouds of dirt. Far ahead, the prairie dog with the flag dove into the ground. The Descenders came to a sudden stop, and Tameron dropped to his knees and shoved his arm into the hole, all the way up to his shoulder. When he pulled out his empty hand, the Descenders began to walk in circles, scanning other holes.

The scouts leaped over prairie dogs like miniature hurdles and quickly caught up to the four teenagers.

To Noah, Sam said, "There's no way you can win this. You know that, right?"

Noah shrugged. "We'll see."

Prairie dogs were racing around in zigzags, diving in and out of the holes. None carried the flag. Noah considered the sweeping web of tunnels beneath them and realized the flag could be anywhere across the prairie by now.

Sam suddenly took off running. He smacked his wrists against his hips and raised his arms out to his sides, opening zippers across his jacket. Feathers spilled out from their leathery confines and fell neatly into place across his back. At the same time, thin telescopic rods shot out from the ends of his sleeves, spreading more feathers. In only a few seconds, his wings were complete, and the Descender jumped into flight. Twenty feet above, he hunted for the flag, his flapping wings stirring up dust.

Taking Sam's lead, Hannah tugged the pull-loops on her boots, and her thick soles swelled to five times their original size. She sprang forward, crossing twenty feet to where a prairie dog had just poked its head up from a hole. She landed, a cloud of dirt swirling up around her legs, and plucked the prairie dog out of its hole. She checked for the flag, saw it wasn't there, and dropped the animal. Then she lunged to another distant spot and scanned the holes.

"Real fair . . ." Richie said.

Tameron, standing nearby, heard this. "Kid . . . fare is for the bus."

Noah stared overhead as Sam flew by. Coasting on wide wings, the Descender looked like something out of a fairy tale. His long silver feathers fluttered as he flapped his arms a single time, creating a gust of wind that raised dust and scattered prairie dogs.

"Noah!"

Noah turned to see Richie on his knees, his arm buried to his shoulder in a hole. His big glasses lay in the dirt. "A little help over here?"

Noah rushed over. "What are you doing?"

"My arm!" He kept his scream to a whisper. "A prairie dog popped up with the flag! I tried to grab it and *this* happened!" He pulled back to show how his arm wouldn't budge.

Noah squatted down. "What do you want me to do? Pull?"

"I sure don't want you to *push*!"

Noah eased in behind Richie and wrapped his arms around his waist. "I'll pull on the count of three," Noah said. "You push. Got it?"

Richie nodded.

"One . . ."

Noah braced himself, planting one foot.

"Two . . ."

He tightened his grip.

"Three!"

He squeezed and pulled, and Richie's arm popped out like the cork from a champagne bottle. The boys shot backward and fell into a heap, their arms and legs entwined. A few prairie dogs crept up and sniffed Noah's cheek and Richie's rear end.

The ground around Noah suddenly shook. He tipped his head back to see a pair of purple leather boots— platform boots with huge, ten-inch soles. Hannah. From his position on the ground, Hannah's bright red bangs seemed to be cascading down her face. She smirked and said, "That's certainly the first time a Crosser's been outwitted by a prairie dog."

Before Noah could respond, something exploded from the ground about thirty feet to his left. What looked like a cloud, Noah realized, were butterflies, thousands of them. Different sizes and patterns, they flew in erratic paths, weaving through one another as they streamed from a three-feet-wide hole in the ground, their wings snapping color across the blue canvas of the sky.

"No way . . ." Richie marveled.

More and more butterflies filled the air. Prairie dogs scattered and flashed their round rear ends as they dove into holes. As Sam flew over the butterflies, his wings drew them across his body and the Descender seemed to burst with reds and blues and yellows.

"What are they doing?" Richie asked.

Hannah stood with her hands on her hips, perfectly calm. "It's a handoff."

"Huh?"

Before Hannah could answer, a prairie dog jumped out of the ground with the flag in his mouth. He took a few steps toward the hole with the butterflies and dropped the flimsy flag inside it. The butterflies immediately reversed direction and disappeared back into the hole. Within seconds they were gone, and so was the flag.

Sam touched down and folded his wings across his back. To his friends, he said, "Let's go!" and fell feetfirst into the butterfly's hole. Tameron and Solana chased after him. Hannah lifted her eyebrows at the scouts and allowed a big bubble to burst against her face. With the quick lap of her tongue, she wiped away the residue, then dove more than twenty feet through the air and disappeared headfirst into the hole, leaving the scouts alone with the prairie dogs.

"Wow," Richie said after a few seconds. He picked up his glasses and planted them squarely on his face. "That kind of stuff—you know, the earth exploding with butterflies—it never really stops impressing me."

Noah said, "You know where that tunnel goes, right?"

"My guess is the Secret Butterfly Nets."

Noah nodded. They ran to the hole and stared into it. A wave of fear crossed over Noah. The scouts had never been to the sector attached to the butterfly house in the Clarksville Zoo. For them, this was uncharted ground.

"What do we do?" Richie asked.

"Exactly what the Descenders did. We jump in."

"And what if we go *splat* on the other side?"

"We won't."

"How do you know?"

"Think about it, Richie. Butterfly *Nets*."

Richie's jaw fell as he realized what Noah was getting at.

Marlo suddenly touched down on Noah's shoulder.

"You're just in time," Noah said to the kingfisher. "Tell Ella and Megan there's been a change of plans—we're headed to the Secret Butterfly Nets!"

Marlo glanced into the big hole, chirped once, then flew into the air.

Noah turned to Richie and said, "C'mon—we got a flag to catch."

One at a time, they jumped feetfirst into the hole, leaving Little Dogs of the Secret Prairie behind.

CHAPTER 17

MARLO LEADS THE WAY

Crossing the Secret Kangaroo Kampground was no problem for Ella and Megan. They'd trained in here dozens of times and knew the best way across it. Over a forested campground sat hundreds of tents with velvet flaps for entrance doors. Used to test the magic for gateways throughout the Secret Zoo, the tents portaled to one another. The quickest path across the sector involved using the best combination of portals. Ella and Megan magically made their way across in a matter of minutes.

As the girls stepped through the magical divide into the City of Species, they immediately spotted Blizzard. The coal-black tip of his long snout twitched and wriggled as he pulled the familiar scents of Ella and Megan out of the air. He lowered his rump and the girls climbed on, Ella in the forward spot.

Ella said, "Take us to Little Dogs of the Secret Prairie!"

The polar bear softly growled and headed off down the street. But he only got a few feet before Marlo swooped down from the treetops and landed on his snout, chirping wildly. Blizzard stopped and paid attention. Then the kingfisher jumped into a new direction in the air and the big bear followed.

"What's going on?" Ella asked. "Why are we turning?"

"Looks like there's been a change of plans," Megan answered.

"I hope these guys know what they're doing."

As usual, the City of Species teemed with commotion and excitement. Animals strolled down colorful sidewalks and skipped across branches. Children rode lions and giraffes, and adults, dressed in thin green jackets, marched with clipboards and briefcases.

Blizzard chased Marlo down a wide, dark alley. The polar bear splashed through a shallow river full of fish and turned onto a new street, frightening off a group of skittish emus. He soon stopped at a glass building with ten sides—a decagon. Rising more than a dozen stories into the treetops, its clear panels were framed with steel.

A wide banner read "Sector 77—The Secret Butterfly Nets." Inside, an unimaginable number of butterflies were sweeping across the glass, flashing their vibrant hues.

"That's what a tornado trapped in a crayon factory would look like," Ella pointed out.

Marlo dipped down and landed on Blizzard's head, appearing like a blue bow in his white fur.

The girls turned their stares to the thin strips of velvet hanging at the building's entrance only a few feet away. There was no sign of the flag, the scouts, or the Descenders.

CHAPTER 18

The Secret Butterfly Nets

Noah and Richie fell from the tunnel into an enormous space. Richie kicked at the air, his flashy running shoes leaving momentary streaks of color. Noah touched down on a large, flat net and quickly rolled aside to make room for his friend, who landed with a grunt. After climbing to his knees on the cords, Noah stared out.

They were in a tall glass building the length of a football field. A wild mesh of nets filled the otherwise open space, running in all directions and angles and connecting in all sorts of ways. They reminded Noah of the climbing nets in playgrounds and parks. Some rose like ladders, while others lay flat. Some sagged, and others were pulled tight. Some angled and curved like the steep corners of a race-track, and others just dangled from the heights.

"No way," Noah said.

He'd never seen a sector so crowded. There were tens of thousands of butterflies—maybe hundreds of thousands. They flew all around, their gentle wings whisking against his body. They flitted through the nets and perched on their cords. The air seemed to be exploding with silent fireworks.

About thirty yards to Noah's left, the Descenders were climbing down a vertical net, chasing a group of butter-flies. In their midst, the thin flag fluttered and snapped like a magician's handkerchief. The butterflies swept beneath the edge of a cargo net and began to fly straight, taking the flag with them. The Descenders jumped onto horizontal nets and charged on their feet after them.

Richie was lying on his stomach, his back covered in butterflies. He lifted his head and revealed the faint impression of a rope across his face. When a butterfly struck one lens of his glasses, he flinched and his arms slipped between the cords.

"A little help . . ." he said, his arms dangling beneath him.

Noah grabbed Richie's jacket and hoisted him up among a scatter of butterflies. Richie looked out across the sector and neatly summed up the scene: "Wow . . ."

Noah pointed toward the Descenders and said, "C'mon—the flag's that way."

They stood and jogged along the net, careful not to let their feet slip through the holes. Butterflies began to land on Noah, one after another. He saw the orange spots of monarchs and the black-and-white stripes of swallowtails.

The butterflies with the flag had shifted directions and were flying back into the heights. The Descenders, climbing now on a vertical net that resembled the rope rigging on the mast of a pirate ship, were closing fast on them, Solana in the lead. Noah saw how the net that he and Richie were on continued straight for about thirty yards before ending at an open space surrounding the net their adversaries were scaling, and he suddenly had an idea. Maybe he and Richie wouldn't need to reach the flag first.

"Richie, I need you to follow me as fast as you can!"

"What for?"

"To grab the flag. Just stop when I don't."

Before Richie could ask another question, Noah charged forward. He fought to keep his balance on the wobbly rope, his ankles turning and twisting. Butterflies peeled off him like a layer of fine snow. As the end of the net grew near, Noah stared up to see Solana reaching out for the flag. Perfect timing. He launched himself into the air, his arms and legs stretched in opposite directions, and touched down on the vertical net, sending tremors across its corded reaches. Solana's feet slipped out from under her just as she snatched the flag, and she fell, one hand holding the flimsy fabric, the other grabbing at the air.

Noah clung to the swaying net and stared back at the one he'd just jumped from. Richie was standing at its edge.

"Here it comes, Richie!"

His friend's eyes opened wide as he realized what Noah wanted.

Butterflies swirled around Solana as she fell through the open space between the two scouts. At just the right moment, Richie swept out his arm and plucked away the flag in a one-in-a-million grab. The Descender plunged another twenty feet and landed safely in the soft sag of a net below.

Richie stared at his capture, his mouth an oval of surprise. The other Descenders had seen what had happened and were now climbing down, looking very unhappy.

Noah searched the distance for the gateway to the City of Species. Through the ropes and the swarming masses of butterflies, he spotted it. In the core of the building dangled a velvet curtain that was shredded into thin strips and adorned with the orange-and-black patterns of a monarch butterfly.

"Richie—the city gateway!"

Richie stared beneath him. "So?"

"So, *go!*"

Noah jumped off to the side and landed on an angled net several feet beneath them. Richie followed. They ran twenty feet, dove through the air, and went into a roll on the sharp slope of a new net. As they came to rest in a sagging area, Noah snatched the flag from Richie and stuffed it into his jacket pocket. Then they crawled to an edge, tossed themselves over, and dropped several feet to another net, this one pitched at a gentler angle. They climbed to their feet and ran again.

Noah glanced above him to see the Descenders were gaining fast, jumping calmly from net to net, as if they knew the best path to get to the scouts. Noah leaped to a rope wall that dangled in an open channel between the other nets. Richie did the same. As they climbed down, the Descenders split up to cut them off.

"Move!" Noah commanded.

Butterflies continued to swarm around them. They clung to their clothes and swept their wings against their bare skin. As the city gateway drew close, Noah realized its only access big enough for them was through a tunnel-like net that branched out to different areas—the entrance to one branch was just several feet down from the scouts and across the open channel.

The rope wall violently shook. Noah and Richie peered over their heads to see that Sam had landed on their net. He quickly jumped off, raised his wings, and started to coast down through the open space.

Noah quickened his pace, chanting, *"Move, move, move!"*

Just as the scouts reached the rope tunnel leading to the gateway, Sam dropped down in front of them, blocking their passage. With his wings fanning the air, the Descender hovered like a hummingbird. Gusts of wind stirred butterflies and snapped the earflaps on Noah's cap. The scouts clung to the wall of rope as it began to sway.

"Almost," Sam said with a proud smirk. "Now . . . hand over the flag."

Noah said nothing. His eyes shifted as he contemplated his options.

"C'mon . . . ," said Sam, "you didn't actually expect to beat us, did you, kid?"

Noah thought about this and decided he had.

Sam's irritation began to show. "Don't make me take it from you. It'll hurt more than your feelings if I do."

Noah reached into his jacket pocket and slowly pulled out the flag. Maybe it was best to end it here, before someone got hurt.

"That's it," Sam said.

Noah glanced at the flag in his hand and noticed

something. His arm was buried in butterflies. An idea struck him.

"Richie . . ." Noah whispered from the corner of his mouth.

"Huh?"

"Get ready."

Sam seemed to sense Noah was up to something because he said, "Don't try anything stupid, kid. Just toss over that flag and this—"

But before he could finish, Noah pulled back his arm and whipped it forward as if he were throwing a baseball. Dozens of butterflies slipped off his sleeve and flew straight at Sam, who turned his head, his eyes closed.

"Richie—go!"

Noah kicked off the rope wall and dove forward, directly beneath Sam's right wing. Long silver feathers brushed across his body, and then Noah landed inside the rope tunnel. Richie followed, diving under Sam's left wing and touching down next to Noah. Sam swatted away the butterflies and spun around to face the scouts just as they crawled off.

"*Go!*" Noah commanded.

Their wrists twisted and their fingers tangled in the cords, but they didn't slow their pace. As they closed to within thirty feet of the gateway, Noah glanced back to see that all four of the Descenders had made their way into the tunnel and were now chasing after them.

Richie's arms slipped through the rope floor, and as Noah stopped to help him up, the Descenders gained on them.

The scouts took off again. The curtain came to within twenty feet, fifteen feet. When they were ten feet away from the gateway, the tunnel grew wider and taller and they clambered up to their feet. Seconds later, the two of them held out their arms and pushed through the loose velvet strips.

CHAPTER 19

THE BIG WHITE RUMP

As Sam charged through the curtain, he slammed into something and stopped with a painful jolt. Hannah crashed into his backside, then Solana and Tameron. Together, the Descenders fell to the rope floor on top of one another. Sam stared up. Protruding through the gateway was the wide, white rump of a polar bear.

"Blizzard," he grumbled.

Blizzard's stubby tail wagged, surely in amusement, then the velvet pieces slipped off the curves of his big bottom as he stepped back into the City of Species.

The Descenders untangled themselves and jumped to

their feet. By the time they stepped into the city, Blizzard and the scouts were already lost in the surrounding crowd. Sam shook his wings and sprinkled butterflies all around.

"That runt," Sam said, thinking of Noah. "All you guys—get into gear."

The Descenders knew what this meant. Solana released her quills. As Tameron reached around with both arms and pulled two zippers along his waist, small plates pushed out from slits in his jacket and fused into a flexible suit of reptile-like armor. He pulled his knit cap over his face and the soft fabric hardened into a helmet that left only his eyes and jaw exposed. Then he yanked a cord on his backpack and out spilled his enormous tail.

"Which way?" Solana asked.

The Descenders scanned the streets and the sidewalks between the towering buildings.

Hannah pointed. "There!"

From an alley drifted a winding trail of butterflies.

Without a word, Sam dove into the air. Tameron and Solana raced after him, splitting the crowd of animals. Hannah sprang forward and landed on a high branch. Then she jumped to a tall balcony, scattering a group of possums.

On the streets of the City of Species, the four teenagers did what they did best. They descended.

≪ CHAPTER 20 ≫

DOWN THE ALLEY

Animals jumped out of Blizzard's way as he thundered down the alley, grumbling and growling. On his back, Noah clung to Richie, Richie clung to Megan, Megan clung to Ella, and Ella clung to the sides of Blizzard's neck, her fists full of fur. Large leaves hung down from a thick web of ivy, occasionally skipping off the scouts' heads.

Noah peered back just as the Descenders rounded the corner into the alley, Sam flying, the others on foot. The momentum of their turn swept Tameron's tail up one brick wall, where it shattered a window box. Dirt and flowers exploded into the air. More birds scattered.

"Move, Blizzard!" Noah said. "They're coming!"

Blizzard rounded a sharp turn into a new alley. Richie shrieked. As they charged forward, Noah glanced back again to see the Descenders still after them.

Blizzard made another turn and barreled into the open streets of the City of Species, frightening a group of peacocks away. Nearby was an ornate building with rows of columns and winding flights of steps. A flag read "Sector 67—The Secret Rhinorama." Blizzard charged for its gateway. Seconds before the curtain swept across Noah, he peered back. The Descenders had emerged from the alley just in time to see where they had gone.

CHAPTER 21

A RUSH OF RHINOS

Blizzard charged onto a grassy plain with low hills and sparse woodlands: a savannah. A view from above would have revealed the polar bear as a lively white speck on a green sprawl. Winds bowed branches and patches of tall grass. The barrenness of the sector reminded Noah of Little Dogs of the Secret Prairie, but there was one major difference: this sector was crowded with one-ton animals with deadly horns. Far across the savannah, a blinking light marked the gateway back to the Clarksville Zoo.

Noah peered over his shoulder to see the Descenders

push through the curtain less than thirty yards away. "Blizzard—they're coming!"

The polar bear growled his understanding and picked up speed.

As Noah continued to stare back, Sam raised his wings and flew forward, quickly crossing the distance to the scouts.

"Get down!" Noah called out.

His friends dropped like dominoes across Blizzard's back, and Sam swept above them, nearly knocking them off.

Across the savannah, the rhinos began to stir. Some of them followed their curiosity a few cautious steps toward the commotion.

Hannah crouched and sprang forward. She landed directly behind Blizzard and swung her arm at Noah, just missing.

Noah looked forward. The gateway was barely visible. "We're not going to make it!"

As Sam dove at them again, Blizzard dodged to one side, eluding him. Seconds later, a rhino charged up alongside the scouts. The enormous animal had an especially large horn, and Noah recognized him immediately: Little Bighorn. He swung his bulky body closer to Blizzard, as if to help protect the scouts.

Noah noticed a gradual hill to their left. Beyond it, he saw the uppermost branches of a wooded area. Then he saw the treetops for what they could provide them. Cover. Protection from Sam.

He shook Richie's shoulder and then pointed to the hillside. "That way!"

Richie looked over and seemed to understand. He nudged Megan and forced her attention to what Noah had shown him. Then Megan elbowed Ella and did the same. Ella nodded, then swatted the left side of Blizzard's neck, a signal to turn.

The polar bear veered off the direct path to the gateway with Little Bighorn still at his side. As Blizzard charged over the hill and down a slope, a ravine appeared. Lined with leafy trees, it followed a winding river, and rhinos packed its lush landscape. Standing side by side, they chewed on grass and kick-splashed through the water.

Blizzard and Little Bighorn abruptly turned in their former direction.

"Looks like we're not going in there!" Ella said.

"The heck we're not!" Noah countered. "Ella—turn us back!"

"What?" Ella shouted. "Are you nuts!"

"Just do it!"

Ella seemed to consider this a moment, then reached over and clapped her palm against the side of Blizzard's neck. The polar bear rolled back his snout, grunted, and continued forward, ignoring her request.

"*C'mon, Blizzard!*" Noah called out from his back seat. "*Trust me!*"

Just when it seemed Blizzard wouldn't heed Noah's command, he and Little Bighorn veered back toward the water.

As the ravine came closer and closer, the rhinos in the large herd turned in Blizzard's direction. Noah looked to his friends and saw nothing more than the backs of their heads: Ella's ponytail whipping around; Richie's pom-pom rolling and quaking; Megan's pigtails flapping like a puny pair of wings.

"Hold on!" Noah commanded.

The scouts squeezed one another as they pierced the herd. Blizzard bumped into one rhino, then another, and another. Little Bighorn did the same. Both animals turned to follow the river, and a few startled rhinos took off in the same direction. Then others did. Then more and more until all the nearby rhinos were charging along with them.

In the grassy ravine, Blizzard and Little Bighorn had intentionally started a stampede.

The ground quaked and the rumble of hooves became a deafening roar. Noah's vision blurred as he was jolted left and right. Other than trees, there was almost nothing to see but the backs of rhinos and their huge horns stabbing skyward. Mud and water splashed through the gaps between their bodies.

Noah glanced back and saw that his idea was working. Because of the trees, Sam could no longer spot them from the air. Having lost sight of the scouts, the Descenders were toward the back of the stampede.

Somewhere in front of Blizzard, a series of loud, long cracks erupted. A few rhinos had accidentally plowed into a batch of trees, toppling them onto the stampede. The trees rolled and tumbled down the backs of the rhinos, their smaller branches snapping and spiraling like batons into the heights. As one trunk reached Blizzard, the mighty polar bear thrust up his head and flung it into the air, high above the scouts.

All at once the stampede shifted direction and started up the hillside. The scouts were soon back on the smooth stretch of land headed toward the portal, a colorful curtain magically swinging from thin air. At least fifty yards back, the Descenders followed. Once the trees opened again, Sam took to the air and immediately spotted the scouts.

Noah chanted for Blizzard to *go go go!*

As the gateway came to within thirty yards, the rhinos at the front of the stampede swerved to avoid it. The curtain closed to within twenty yards . . . ten yards . . . five . . . three . . . one.

And then Blizzard and the scouts were gone.

CHAPTER 22

And the Winner Is . . .

Blizzard emerged into the Rhinorama exhibit inside a concrete cave and quickly carried the scouts out into the airy night, where the Clarksville Zoo was still almost pitch-black. He plodded across the exhibit's open yard, jumped the narrow concrete moat along its perimeter, and headed up a path. As he rounded Ostrich Island, Noah peered over his shoulder and spotted the Descenders. In Rhinorama, they were splitting off in different directions toward the scouts.

"They're still on us!" Noah shouted.

Blizzard lowered his head and picked up speed, his

weighty paws pounding the asphalt. He veered off through a yard, jumped the long rails of the Fast Train Through Clarksville, and circled the Forest of Flight. When they reached ZOOasis, Blizzard headed straight for the vase that Tank had set on the path, and Noah plucked the flag from his pocket and readied himself to drop it in. Nearby, Tank and Mr. Darby were seated on a marble bench.

Tank stood and started to clap. "Bring it home!"

Noah and Richie both peered over their shoulders. Solana was the only one behind them, her long quills dangling off her jacket. The other Descenders were nowhere in sight.

"Where'd they go?" Richie gasped.

Just beyond the vase, Tameron appeared in the flower-bed, dry stalks crunched beneath his stretched-out tail. Then, twenty feet off the path to the scouts' left, Hannah suddenly came down out of the air and landed in a crouch, her red bangs masking her eyes.

"Hurry, Bliz!" Megan yelled.

The vase came into full view, moonlight glinting off its curves. As Blizzard ran beside it, Noah leaned over, reached out his arm, and dropped the flag as close as he could to its mouth. The thin velvet softly fell a few inches, then abruptly took off in a new direction—straight down the path toward Tameron, fluttering like a tiny magic carpet in a wild wind. As it neared the flowerbed, Tameron swept around his tail and somehow snatched it out of the air. It wasn't until his tail dropped still onto the ground that exactly what had happened was revealed. The flag was pinned to his armored append-age with a single quill, one that Solana had pitched from behind the scouts.

Before the scouts could do anything, Tameron raised his tail high and Sam flew over his head, tearing the flag from the quill. He then swooped directly over the vase, stuffed the flag inside, and touched down on the path beside Solana.

Noah stared in disbelief at the Descenders. Solana and Sam bumped fists. Hannah raised her eyebrows, blew a softball-size bubble, and allowed it to burst against her lips—an odd, victory *pop*!

"That's cheating!" Richie said. "They can't win like that!"

Mr. Darby rose from the bench, stepped up to Blizzard, and stroked the bear's head. He turned his smile to the scouts. "I'm afraid they can. The Descenders—they are very resourceful. They will always be tough to beat."

"But—" Richie stammered. "The flag was like . . . *right there*!"

Mr. Darby said, "Closer than anyone expected, I assure you."

As Sam folded his wings across his back, he wordlessly walked past the scouts and clapped hands with Tameron. Blizzard growled in bitterness.

"It's . . . not fair," Richie added.

Hannah plucked the flag from the vase, walked up to the scouts, and tossed the flag to Richie. "Here. Something for those tears."

Richie clenched the flag in his fist and shook it toward Hannah. "I got a *better* idea!"

Hannah smirked and smacked her gum. "Yeah?"

"Why don't I . . ." His eyes shifted back and forth. "How about I . . ."

The scouts watched Richie with hopeful expressions. Maybe he could find words that might ease the terrible sting of this moment.

"I . . ." A long pause. "Forget it. I can't think of a single witty thing to say. It's like someone parked a truck on my brain."

Hannah smiled. "Maybe next time, kid." She playfully punched his leg and walked off, adding, "But probably not."

Ella leaned back toward Richie. "Thanks a lot, dude. I feel *way* cooler now."

The Descenders joined Tank and Mr. Darby and then retracted their gear. As Tameron's armor spread apart and slipped away, his tail coiled back into his canvas pack.

"It still blows my mind," Megan said as she watched the Descenders. "It's like they're superheroes."

"And it's like we're super*zeroes*," Ella groaned.

Tank and the Descenders walked off together. As Mr. Darby turned to leave, he waved his hand for the scouts to follow. "Come—we have something to show you."

"Show us?" Richie muttered.

Noah glanced at his friend and shrugged his shoulders. "Guess we'll find out."

"Don't we always?" Ella asked.

Blizzard plodded forward into the new unknown.

☙ CHAPTER 23 ❧

THE CAMPOUT IN THE
FOREST OF FLIGHT

Near the middle of the zoo, the group reached the Forest of Flight, a forty-feet-high birdhouse with a domed roof made of glass. Overhead, starlight sparkled on the clear, curved panes. As the Descenders pushed through the entrance, they held open the doors for the scouts, who were still perched high on Blizzard. All the scouts thought to duck except for Richie, who clunked his head on the doorway's metal frame.

The open exhibit allowed people to walk among freely flying birds. The air was scented with the earthy aroma of soil and tree bark. Trees and flowery plants helped fill the space, and waterfalls spilled down rocky walls, bursting into mist along the way. Birds flew overhead and wove among branches. A medley of sounds ricocheted off the hard walls—water splashing, streams rumbling, and birds chirping and squawking.

"This way, everyone!" Mr. Darby called as he headed down a misty path that ran beside a tall rock formation made of concrete.

As Blizzard rounded the turn, the scouts came upon an incredible sight. A crowd of animals was gathered around a series of picnic benches. Covered with decorative cloths, the tables held cakes and cookies and ice cream. Ribbons and pennants dangled from the heights, and helium balloons were tied to benches, beams, and branches. Birds pulled long, colorful streamers through the air. Tied between two trees, an overhead banner read, "Congratulations, scouts!"

Ella turned to Mr. Darby. "Uhhh . . . in case you haven't heard, we lost."

"Only the lesser contest," Mr. Darby said.

Ella scrunched up her face. "Huh?"

"You've been members of the Secret Society—Crossers—for a full year!"

With DeGraff moving on the Clarksville Zoo, Noah hardly thought it was a time for a celebration, and he told Mr. Darby so. The old man nodded in understanding, but said, "We must celebrate our triumphs—even more so in the face of such danger."

"Makes sense to me," Richie said as he eyed the treats on the tables. "Especially when there's cake involved."

Mr. Darby continued, "Besides, the zoo is fully guarded tonight, and we must give our trust to others in the Secret Society—our success depends on it."

Blizzard lowered his rump and the scouts climbed off. As they headed down the path, the Descenders stepped up to congratulate them.

"Nice," Sam said to Noah, clapping him on the shoulder as Noah walked past.

"Good work, kid," Tameron said.

Hannah popped a bubble and playfully pushed the side of his head.

When Noah reached Solana, she winked at him. Noah thought to wink back and nervously decided against it. Instead, a smile found his lips.

Just beyond the Descenders was Tank. As the scouts walked by the big man, he held his fist out to each one of them, saying, "All right . . . all right, now," and the four friends took turns punching his knuckles.

Most of the animals were ones the scouts had adventured with in the Secret Zoo. Dozens of prairie dogs raced about, curiously sniffing at things in their erratic paths: the grass, the tree trunks, the posts of steel railings.

Chickadees weaved through streamers and perched along the interior landscape. Hummingbirds zipped back and forth and hovered, their needlelike beaks probing at flowers. Among several otters was Louie, with whom Noah had shared a Wotter Tower slide a year ago. And Marlo was in attendance, perched on a jug of lemonade.

Noah felt something poke his shoulder and turned to find Podgy, his flippers pressed flat against his bulbous body. Noah reached out and patted the emperor penguin's large head.

"Come!" Mr. Darby said as he waved the scouts over to the picnic tables. "Please, let's have dessert."

Their group stepped cautiously through the prairie dog coterie and took seats at the tables. From across one bench seat, a portly prairie dog scampered up to Richie. P-Dog.

"Hey, you," Richie said. He scooped him up and set him on the tabletop so the other scouts could take turns scratching his head.

"Is he still hurt?" Noah asked no one in particular.

Ella shrugged her shoulders and not-so-gently poked his side. "Seems okay to me."

Tank cut the cake, Hannah scooped ice cream, and Mr. Darby passed out the plates. The scouts dug in. As Richie crammed cake into his mouth, he smeared chocolate across his face like war paint. This was much to the distaste of Ella, who wrinkled her nose and asked if he'd be more comfortable with a bowl on the ground. The Descenders also found seats. Noah couldn't get over how strange it felt to see the teenagers eating cake and ice cream when, just minutes ago, they'd chased the scouts across the Secret Zoo in their magical forms. As they ate, Mr. Darby asked about the game, and the Crossers shared their stories, sometimes breaking into laughter.

As Ella served herself a second piece of cake, an unexpected visitor crawled onto the bench and took a seat beside her. Ko. The koala pointed her beady eyes and coal-black snout at Ella.

"What's up, Ko?" Ella said with a smile as she scratched the spot between the koala's round ears. Then she sliced off a piece of cake with her fork and poked it toward the animal. "Want some?"

Ko gave her fork a sniff, then wrinkled her nose and promptly pulled her head away.

"No worries," Ella said. "I feel the same way about eucalyptus leaves."

Solana was sitting on the opposite side of the table from Noah. He saw her high cheekbones, her dark eyes, her full lips. As he watched, Solana lifted her long hair off her shoulders and tossed it onto her back, revealing the skin of her neck like a secret. Her eyes suddenly shifted over to Noah, and she caught him staring at her.

Noah quickly looked away, blushing.

After the cake was gone, the scouts left the table to spend time with their animal friends. Ella invited Ko to climb on her back, and the two of them broke off from the group to roam the exhibit, walking through streamers as they gazed around. Richie spent time with the prairie dogs, wrestling with them on the ground like a giant litter of puppies. Megan strolled through the trees, inviting hummingbirds and chickadees to perch on her fingers.

Noah played a version of tag with Louie that he only half understood. He'd chase the otter around until Louie decided he didn't want to be chased anymore, at which point he'd run after Noah. Marlo kept perched on Noah's shoulder the entire time.

When Noah chased Louie around a big boulder, he came upon Solana. She sat on a bench beside the winding walkway. Across from her was a concrete wall with holes that provided places for the birds to build nests—and to get to the Secret Zoo. When Solana saw him, he immediately stopped chasing Louie and straightened up. He suddenly felt like a fool—Solana had just caught him goofing around with an otter.

Solana said, "This is really the place that started it all for you, isn't it?"

"Huh?"

"The holes." She tipped her head toward the wall. "The time when the birds came out and surrounded you. That was when this all started—for the scouts, I mean."

Noah thought about this. "Yeah, I guess so. But how do you know about that?"

Solana grinned. "The Secret Zoo . . . it's really not such a big place. Word spreads pretty quick."

With Marlo still on his shoulder, Noah stood in silence, feeling stupid and not understanding why. Solana glanced at him. Twice. Three times.

"Why don't you sit down?" she said at last, her stare fixed on the wall. "You're making me nervous just standing there."

Noah looked around for a place to sit. The only vacant spot was the one next to Solana. Was she inviting him to sit beside her? So . . . *close*?

Solana glanced back again. "I don't bite," she said. "Not often, anyway."

Realizing how foolish he was acting, Noah rushed over and dropped down on the bench—a bit too firmly, however, as Solana shook, and Marlo chirped and ruffled his feathers in surprise.

"Oops," Noah said. "Sorry."

Solana smiled. "You talking to me or the bird?"

He didn't know what to say. He turned to her and smiled back.

Solana lifted her gaze to the top of Noah's head. "Where did you get that thing?"

"Huh?" Noah asked. "My . . . head?"

Solana's smile widened. "Your *hat*."

"Oh," Noah said. "The Secret Zoo. Arctic Town. The animals . . . they gave it to me."

Solana continued to stare at the hat. Her silence made him uncomfortable.

Noah said, "Is there something wrong with it?"

Solana shook her head. "It's just kind of goofy. It makes you look like a little kid."

The thought worried him. He could suddenly feel the hat on his head—its weight, the press of its poofy insulation, the dangle of its droopy earflaps. He'd never cared about what it looked like; he'd simply appreciated its warmth and comfort. Now he hated it. He wanted to rip it off his head and chuck it into a hole in the wall, sending it back to the Secret Zoo.

Solana reached for his hat and paused. "Can I?" When Noah didn't object, she stripped off the cap and dropped it on his lap. Then, with a quick sweep of her hand, she lifted Noah's long bangs out of his eyes. Noah became acutely aware of her touch and a strange, sudden panic coursed through him.

"There," she said. "Better."

Ella suddenly strolled past with Ko and spotted Noah

sharing the bench with Solana. She stopped, raised an eyebrow, and very loudly said, "Are you kidding me?" before walking off.

"What was that all about?" Solana asked.

"Beats me," Noah lied. "She's weird sometimes."

"Sometimes?"

"Maybe all the time, I guess."

Solana laughed and playfully swatted Noah's leg. Then she rose from the bench and said, "I'm going to check on Hannah," and walked off. As Noah watched her go, he recalled the way her touch on his leg had felt—the way it had made his skin tingle and his insides churn.

Ella jumped out from behind a nearby rock wall. "Please tell me you don't have a crush on that chick."

Noah sat up with a jolt and felt his face flush. "*What?* You got to be—"

"She's too old for you," Ella reminded him. "And she lives in another world. And she has quills . . . you know . . . like a porcupine."

"We were . . . *talking!*" Noah protested.

"Uh-huh," Ella said skeptically. She turned and walked off in the same direction as Solana, her ponytail slapping her shoulders in a way that seemed to show her disapproval. Noah rose from the bench, put on his hat, and followed her, careful to stay back far enough to not invite any more conversation.

Back at the camp, Noah rejoined the others, and over the next half hour, the animals began to fall asleep. The prairie dogs curled into balls, and the chickadees huddled in the trees. Blizzard slept on his stomach, his hind legs perched high and his cold snout buried in his outstretched paws. Podgy dozed on his feet, his bill tucked against the side of his body. The hummingbirds perched on the branches, their feathers fluffed out.

When Mr. Darby announced it was time to get some rest, the Descenders walked off and returned with sleeping bags, backpacks, and pillows, which they tossed to the scouts. They divided into two groups—boys and girls—and changed into pajamas on opposite sides of a tall concrete rock formation. Tank and the Descenders headed back wearing baggy sweats and tight T-shirts. Noah, Ella, and Megan wore loose-fitting, two-piece pajamas. Mr. Darby wore velvet pajamas, slippers, and his dark sunglasses.

As Ella unrolled her sleeping bag, she smiled at Mr. Darby and said, "Whoa—Mr. D in pj's! There's something I never thought I'd see!"

"I consider it sleepwear," Mr. Darby said with a grin. "Comfortable, but dignified."

Noah found it bizarre that Mr. Darby still wore his sunglasses. Just as he readied a question about it, Richie returned to the site and distracted him. His friend was dressed in one-piece, footed pajamas. They were as shockingly red as his winter hat, which he still had on. Embarrassment washed over Noah: his best friend looked like a young, freshly shaven Santa Claus. Noah glanced at Solana. She was giggling and softly shaking her head.

As Richie walked over to his friends with his sleeping bag tucked under his arm, Ella leaned over and whispered, "Honestly—you couldn't go one night without the footsies?"

"What's the big deal?" Richie asked. "You want my toes to get cold?"

He unrolled his sleeping bag between Noah and Ella. On it was an enormous picture of Han Solo, his big-barreled blaster aimed straight ahead.

"Han Solo . . ." Ella said. "Are you *kidding* me?"

"What?" Richie said, a little hurt. "Han was the only member of the Rebel Alliance that ever really mattered. Besides Chewie, of course."

The scouts lay on top of their sleeping bags: Noah beside Richie, beside Ella, beside Megan. On their backs, they stared into the treetops at the chickadees and hummingbirds, which speckled the branches with color.

As Mr. Darby and the Descenders lay on their sleeping bags, Tank walked off, his mammoth muscles quaking beneath his loose-fitting pajamas. He disappeared behind some trees, then the lights in the Forest of Flight blinked out. With the entire building surrendered to darkness, the night sky beyond the glass dome seemed to light up. Hundreds of stars filled the scouts' view.

"*Whoa . . . ,*" Megan said.

"Totally, totally awesome!" Ella agreed.

"The light that helps us see only blinds us from what is there," Mr. Darby said. "True irony."

Tank returned and dropped into his sleeping bag. The group quickly fell into silence. P-Dog curled into a ball near Richie's legs. Ko crawled up and took a spot between Ella and Megan. Marlo swooped down and perched on Noah's leg.

Blizzard yawned and plodded over to Noah. He lay beside him, his coal-black nose a few feet from Noah's face. Blizzard slid his leg across the grassy floor and stopped his meaty paw just inches from Noah. As Noah placed his palm against it, the bear slid his paw away.

Noah twitched with surprise. It was as if Blizzard had meant to give Noah's hand a high five. Smiling, Noah closed his eyes. Within minutes his rambling thoughts settled on Solana. He saw her face, her eyes, her skin. He saw her flip her long, dark hair over her shoulder. He felt her touch.

After a few deep breaths, Noah fell asleep. As he did, he brought Solana—his first real crush—into the world of his dreams.

CHAPTER 24

THE WEIGHT OF EVIE'S PAST

As the scouts slept beneath the starry view in the Forest of Flight, six young teenage girls walked along the neighborhood streets, the magic of chameleons keeping them in perfect camouflage. They moved like ghosts. Specters. Jordynn was watching the western wall. Elakshi and Lee-Lee, the southern wall. Kaleena, the northern wall. And Evie and Sara, the eastern wall.

Evie didn't like being on the Outside. Everything was different. The smells, the sounds. The air stung her throat, and it had a taste to it, something that came from the smoke that Outsiders poured into the air. And Evie missed the noise of the Secret Zoo, its ceaseless chatter of a thousand species. Birds cawing, elephants trumpeting, snakes hissing, frogs croaking—an endless song of animal voices.

Evie became bored and took a seat on the front of a car. A few chameleons jumped down, and she watched spots on the hood swirl and swell as the magic reptiles adjusted to the new surface.

Something nearby slammed shut and she jumped back to the street, startled. To her right, a middle-aged man stood outside his front door. The porch light revealed a briefcase in his one hand and a steamy mug in the other. He yawned, stretched, then walked down the sidewalk. At the end of his driveway, he headed to his car, which was the one Evie had been sitting on. The Specter backed into the middle of the street and watched, knowing she was invisible to him.

His face was freshly shaven, and he smelled like musk and spices—strange aromas that Outsiders put on their skin. He wore a stiff-looking jacket and an irritated expression: eyebrows pulled down, lips pursed tight. Evie imagined what bothered him. Being forced to wake early? Having to report to work? His brief walk through the cold?

Anger coursed through her. This man hadn't earned the right to be troubled. He couldn't imagine what Evie and the other Specters had been through, the savagery they'd experienced. Outsiders knew nothing of real pain.

As the man walked past, she reached out and tapped the bottom of his mug. Hot coffee splashed over the brim and streamed down his fingers. He dropped his briefcase, switched the mug to his other hand, and shook the heat off his skin. He cursed under his breath and leaned over for his briefcase. As he did, Evie moved behind him and kicked the case, which slid forward about two feet and stopped, still standing on end.

The man lurched back and stared all around.

Evie smiled. Being a Specter could sometimes be fun.

He set his mug on the roof of his car, leaned over, and watched the briefcase, his eyes wide, his mouth in a worried frown. He poked a finger forward, touched the briefcase, then pulled back his hand. Nothing happened. As he reached for the case a second time, Evie kicked it, sliding it forward again.

The man gasped and craned his neck in new directions. All the color had washed from his face. As Evie stepped around him, he turned left and right. He'd sensed Evie—felt her body stir the air.

"Who's there?" he asked. "Is someone . . . there?"

She smiled. Then she turned toward the man, putting the briefcase between her and him. She knew he probably didn't deserve this—but maybe that was the point. Evie, after all, hadn't deserved what she'd got.

None of the Specters had.

The man hunched over and rushed for his briefcase, the hard heels of his dress shoes clapping against the pavement. Evie kicked the case as hard as she could. It slid through his legs, toppled over, and spun to a stop at least ten feet behind the car.

The man's bottom lip trembled. He lurched toward the rear of the car, tripping over his own feet. Forgetting about his briefcase, he ran for his driveway, his limbs flailing like a string puppet's. He kept glancing over his shoulder, his face frozen in fear, then pushed through his front door, sheltering himself from the unknown thing in the darkness. Evie. The leader of the Specters.

‿❧ CHAPTER 25 ❧‿

HALLS ON HALLOWEEN

For two weeks, things continued as planned. The scouts were able to fit in three more crosstrainings, strictly classroom stuff. The animals and Descenders kept up their nightly patrols, and the Specters moved through the scouts' neighborhood in their magical camouflage. DeGraff wasn't spotted again.

Now it was Halloween night, and Noah and Megan were headed down their street toward Clarksville Elementary with plans to pick up Ella and Richie on the way. The Halloween party at their school was scheduled from six to seven o'clock, at which point the residents of Clarksville would light their jack-o'-lanterns, turn on their porch lights, and invite kids to accept candy at their front doors.

Megan was wearing a pirate costume: a black skirt with a large skull-and-crossbones emblem, a leather belt tied above one hip, tall black boots, a plastic sword, an eye patch, and a thick silver necklace and plenty of silver bracelets. Noah was dressed as a soldier in a desert camouflage uniform—cargo pants and a loose-fitting jacket. He'd streaked camouflage paint over his cheeks and the bridge of his nose, and he also carried a plastic machine gun.

At Richie's house, Richie ran across the lawn to join his friends. He was dressed in a white, collared shirt; checkered pants pulled high above his waist; black shoes; and a large black bow tie. He'd wrapped a wad of white tape around the middle of his glasses. His shirt pocket bulged with pens, pencils, highlighters, a short steel ruler—he'd even added a plastic pocket protector. "Ta-da!" he said, his arms out to his sides. "Mega-nerd!" He ran his thumbs beneath the waist of his pants. "Check out these things— they practically touch my armpits!"

The three of them laughed their way to Ella's house and stopped at her mailbox, where Ella was waiting. She was dressed as Wonder Woman. Red boots with vertical white stripes. A blue, star-spotted skirt. A red, sleeveless shirt with two gold Ws on the front. A short red cape. A gold headband with a red star. Wide steel bracelets. And a gold rope on her hip—the superhero's Lasso of Truth.

"You look like the flag," Richie said, still laughing. He put his hand to his heart and spoke in a monotone: "I pledge allegiance . . . to your costume . . . and to the United States of America."

Megan playfully pushed Richie aside. "Don't listen to him, Ella—you look totally cool!"

Ella spun the way Wonder Woman does and said, "That twirl—yeah, you guys should probably get used to seeing that." She eyed Megan's costume, then added, "Check out the bling! You go, pirate girl! Arrrrr!"

Megan pulled out her sword and pressed it to Richie's neck, saying, "Avast, ye scallywag!"

As Richie's eyes widened, Ella said, "Who could have known you were born to plunder?"

Megan lowered her sword and took a slight bow.

To Richie, Ella said, "What are you supposed to be?"

Richie pulled his pants up higher, exposing his ankles. "I'm a nerd!"

"Yeah—we know," Ella shot back. "But didn't you want to dress up for Halloween?"

"Oh . . . you should make fun. . . ." Richie said. "Nice bracelets. If they were any bigger, you wouldn't be able to bend your arms."

"Maybe," Ella said. "But check this out." She swatted his shoulder with her left forearm.

"Ow!" Richie groaned.

"They're used to defend against all manners of attack—including verbal."

Richie lowered his eyebrows, pursed his lips, then reached into his bulging pocket and pulled out a pen. He aimed it at Ella, pressed the plunger, and a blue stream of ink sprayed from the tip, wetting her costume.

"Richie!" Ella gasped. With her jaw dropped open, she stared down on the inky mess on her clothes.

"Don't worry!" Richie said. "Disappearing ink! It fades over time."

Ella closed her mouth into a frown. "How *much* time?"

Richie thought about this for a moment. "Ten minutes?"

"That sounded like a guess."

"It's supposed to be funny!" he explained. He lifted the pen to his eyes and slowly read the words on the side of it. "'The Squirt Pen of Merriment. The pen that sprays ink and spreads laughter!'"

"Great," Ella said as she dabbed the ink with her fingertips. "I'll let you know when the merriment kicks in."

As they headed up the street, Ella lassoed Richie's head, Megan batted Ella with her plastic sword, and Noah rolled across the street to do battle with an imaginary army, firing his plastic machine gun and hurling invisible grenades. The magic gold key for the Clarksville Zoo shot out of a pocket in his cargo pants and fell to the street.

"Noah—you're going to lose this!" Megan chided. She snatched up the key and snapped it into a small leather pouch on her pirate belt. "I'll hold on to it tonight."

Noah opened his mouth to protest and then stopped himself, figuring the key was more safe in a pouch with a latch than in a baggy pocket.

By the time they reached their school, Ella declared that Richie was no longer in danger of death by lasso, since the ink had faded on her costume. They pushed through the big double doors of the entrance and nearly crashed into a Transformer and a very young Frankenstein with chocolate smudged over his green cheeks. The principal, a kind old man with narrow bifocals, sat dressed as the Tin Man, his face painted silver and an oil funnel fastened to his head. In his lap was a huge bowl brimming with candy. As the scouts walked by, they wished him a Happy Halloween and stuffed their pockets with miniature Snickers and Milky Ways.

Clarksville Elementary was dressed for Halloween. Streamers dangled from the ceiling and looped around poles. Jack-o'-lanterns lined the halls, glow sticks revealing their carved-out innards. Yarn spiderwebs covered the walls. Even the characters in the "Reading Is Your Key" posters had on witch hats and masks cut out from construction paper. Other than a life-size mummy, some bony hands reaching out from the lockers, and a few tombstones with the names of upper elementary teachers, there wasn't much to be scared about.

Richie frowned. "Where's all the terror? The severed body parts and stuff? There's not even a hint of carnage here."

Ella said, "I think the school's going with *merry*, not *scary*."

"On Halloween! Can't we save that stuff for the gentler holidays? You know, the ones with turkeys and stuff?"

"Look around, Richie. This place is full of first graders."

Richie glanced around to see SpongeBob SquarePants, a miniature Iron Man, some princesses, and at least five girls dressed as Dora the Explorer.

"Let's check out the gym," Noah said. "It'll have cooler stuff."

The scouts rushed through the halls. Just past the open doors of the gymnasium stood a wide ficus tree decorated as if for Christmas, only with rubbery eyeballs instead of bulbs.

Richie pinched a fake eyeball between two fingers and said, "Now *this* just says Happy Halloween to me!"

Across the huge room, kids were running through an obstacle course, crawling through a haunted maze, and jumping around inside inflatable bounce houses. Smaller games and activities were stationed along the walls: Pin the Stem on the Pumpkin, a candy corn relay race, a skeleton scavenger hunt, and boxes that kids reached inside to guess at their gooey and gross contents.

At the maze, the four friends crawled into the darkness and steered clear of the pop-out-at-you zombies that looked a lot like their teachers in white face paint and smears of eye shadow. They navigated the strange terrain of the obstacle course and then spent time on the inflatables, bouncing off the walls and one another. Noah realized how great it was to be himself again—to not worry about the Shadowist and all the Secret Zoo's problems. Once their foreheads were amply beaded with sweat, they took a break and headed for the punch bowl. As they leaned against the wall to sip their drinks, Wide Walt and his two brainless companions strolled up. Noah tossed his cup into a garbage can and took a step toward Walt, but Ella grabbed his wrist and held him back.

"Don't," she said. "That's what he wants."

"Walt!" a voice rang out.

Their group turned. Standing under the nearby basketball hoop was Mr. Kershen. Dressed as a zombie, he looked meaner than ever. He was the first live corpse that Noah had seen with a full mustache.

"Walter—find somewhere else to stand!" Mr. Kershen said.

"Yeah, Walt*er*," Ella said, emphasizing the *er* because Walt hated his full name. "Park your *wideness* somewhere else."

Walt grunted, gave the scouts a dirty look, and headed out of sight behind an inflatable pirate ship.

"C'mon," Megan said. "Forget about that jerk. Let's just keep away from him."

They headed toward the gym exit as the party came to an end. Students began to spill out onto the concrete courtyard.

The first thing the scouts noticed was a strange, dense fog that had rolled in.

CHAPTER 26

THE PECULIAR FOG

As students poured out of Clarksville Elementary onto the streets, Tank stepped across the Clarksville Zoo, his size twenty-two boots thumping against the concrete. The once-dim day had eased into night. He stared into the outdoor exhibits. Most of the animals were watchful, but quiet. His thoughts were on the children of Clarksville, the way they'd now be roaming the dark streets where DeGraff had been spotted. The idea horrified him.

He rounded Creepy Critters and headed toward the Forest of Flight. On his way, he exchanged nods with a few security guards. Like him, the guards seemed worried.

A tiny bird swept out of the sky and landed on his shoulder. Marlo. The kingfisher was chirping wildly, tipping his head from side to side. Something was wrong.

"What is it?" Tank asked.

Marlo twittered loudly, sprang off the meaty mound of Tank's shoulder, and flew straight ahead. Tank knew what to do. Follow.

The kingfisher led him across a grassy landscape. As they rounded the Forest of Flight, the southern side of the property came into view. Fog covered everything— fog that seemed to originate from somewhere inside the zoo to Tank's far left.

"What—?"

Marlo chirped, as if to respond to Tank's unfinished thought, then flew off. Mist dotted Tank's cheeks and cooled his throat. His movements swirled the cloudy air. The farther he ran, the less he could see. He followed Marlo by listening to his chirps.

PizZOOria came into view. Tank soon stumbled over the tracks of the Fast Train Through Clarksville. At Ostrich Island, the fog was thicker than ever. At Rhinorama, he raced over the bridge above the perimeter trench and followed Marlo across the open yard, where an empty exhibit meant Little Bighorn was in the Secret Zoo. As Tank neared a concrete mountainside set in a natural hill, a voice rose in his headset, startling him.

"Tank? You out there?" It was Charlie Red.

"Roger that."

"You seeing this fog?"

"Yep. I'm with Marlo at Rhinorama. I can barely see a thing."

"I'm along the west wall," Charlie said. "I can see the fog moving over Koala Kastle. It's so thick . . . like the castle's being swallowed!"

Tank's nerves spiked. The west wall was near Clarksville Elementary—close to the students.

"Tank?" Charlie said.

"Yeah?"

"I don't like the looks of this. This fog—it ain't natural. And it's like . . . it's like it's *coming* from the zoo."

Tank became very silent, then said, "The Descenders aren't tuned to our channel right now. Get them. And the guards—get anyone you can."

"I'm on it," Charlie said.

Tank peered at the fake mountainside. Marlo shot out of the fog—a faint spot of color in a world gone gray— and perched on his shoulder, chirping wildly.

"What?" Tank asked. "You see something?"

The kingerfisher dove into the air, touched down on the rocky wall beside the mouth of a cave, and chirped at Tank, who jogged toward him. The fog was so thick now that Tank felt it beading on his bald head and trickling along the ridge of his brow.

The dark cave, which Tank had seen hundreds of times, looked eerie. Remembering his flashlight, Tank plucked it off his belt and aimed its bright beam into the darkness. The cavity was so cloudy that Tank was certain the fog was coming from there.

Into his headpiece, Tank said, "Charlie, you there?"

No answer.

"You got to be kidding me. Charlie—where'd you go?"

And the big man followed his light into the dark recesses of the cave.

CHAPTER 27

TRICK OR TREAT

Outside of Clarksville Elementary, the younger kids found their parents and the older kids found their friends. In groups, they headed toward the foggy neighborhood and its promise of free candy. An uneven chorus of "Trick or treat!" sounded as Jenkins Street was invaded with miniature monsters and superheroes and ballerinas swinging plastic bags and plastic pumpkins.

As the scouts ran from house to house, they cut through lawns, dodged bushes, and squeezed through hedges. On porches, they held open their bags to claim their sugary loot. The fog continued to thicken, but the scouts barely noticed. By eight o'clock, their bags were half full.

As the four friends headed down Phlox Drive, a man ran up to them. Charlie Red. He stopped in front of the scouts.

"Charlie?" Noah said. "What are you—"

"We got a problem," Charlie said.

"What's going on?"

"This fog . . ." Charlie gestured with a sweep of an arm. "It's all over the Clarksville Zoo. We're worried DeGraff might use it to move on us."

The thought sent a wave of panic through Noah—and a splash of shame. The scouts had been running up and down the streets with nothing but candy on their minds. They'd been behaving like children, not like Crossers, not like select individuals pledged to protect the world.

"What do we do?" Megan asked.

"We've already sent the tarsiers out. And the Descenders—they're moving into position. We have—"

"The *Descenders*?" Ella said. "But there are people everywhere! What if—"

"We got no choice!" Charlie said.

Understanding this, the scouts kept quiet.

Charlie continued, "The Specters—they're out, too. And Darby's making sure every possible portal into the Secret Zoo is guarded." Charlie's face changed with a new thought and he said, "You guys have your headsets?"

The four friends shook their heads. Again, Noah felt a bit disgusted at himself.

Charlie reached into his jacket pocket and pulled out four headsets, the sort the scouts had learned to use. "Take these." He threw one to each of the friends. As they fitted them into their ears, Charlie added, "Divide up. If you spot anything, radio it in." Then he turned and ran. Within seconds, he disappeared into the darkness, the misty air swirling in his wake.

The scouts stared at one another. It was Noah who finally broke the silence.

"Let's go."

The scouts split off in different directions, hoping to cover as much ground as possible. Noah found himself glancing all around, suddenly sure DeGraff could be anywhere.

CHAPTER 28

THE HUNT BEGINS

Noah headed down Jenkins Street, which bordered three sides of the Clarksville Zoo, and turned onto Timber Trail, a winding road surrounded by old homes. Tall oaks stretched their mighty limbs across the street, making Timber Trail seem like a tunnel cut through a small forest.

He walked briskly, trying to remain calm and not call attention to himself. Empty-handed, he'd since dropped his bag of candy and toy machine gun. Along the curbs sat jack-o'-lanterns, their expressions seemingly carved out of the darkness rather than the pulpy shells of pumpkins.

Children rushed between houses and chants of "Trick or treat!" sounded from all directions. Adults followed their kids, and wagons carrying costume-clad toddlers rumbled along.

In Noah's head, a sudden thought washed away all others. What if DeGraff was in a costume? He turned to the adults, many of whom were dressed up. He saw a princess, an Indiana Jones, and the grim reaper, the shaft of his scythe propped against his shoulder.

"Man . . . this is not good," Noah said to himself.

"Excuse me?"

Noah looked over to see a man dressed in a beige jumpsuit with a patch of a cartoonish ghost stitched to one shoulder. The ghost was enclosed in a red circle with a diagonal line. A ghostbuster.

"You say something?" the man asked.

"I . . ." Noah's sentence faded away, and he hurried off.

Down the street he went, searching all around. As he neared the end of Timber Trail, he touched the transmit button on his earpiece and said, "Guys—can you hear me?"

When all the scouts answered yes, Noah then asked if anyone had seen anything. "No" was their response.

CHAPTER 29

THE FALSE ALARM

Megan headed down Zinnia Street, which branched from Jenkins to join several other side roads. She scanned the foggy landscape for DeGraff, her plastic sword swinging with her stride.

This is hopeless, she thought.

She saw something then, a dark figure standing between two houses. She halted and peered at it. A man. A man masked in fog and shadow.

"I see something," she whispered, the vibrations in her skull transmitting her voice into the ears of the scouts.

A new voice suddenly came through her speaker:

"What do you got?" It was Tameron, which meant the Descenders had crossed to the Outside and joined their radio channel.

"Someone . . ." Megan said. "I don't know . . . he looks suspicious."

"Roger that," Tameron said. "Sam, you getting this?" Apparently the two were separated. The Descenders had likely divided up, like the scouts.

"Roger," Sam said. "Megan, tell us what you see."

But before Megan could say more, two trick-or-treaters rushed up to the man and led him across a yard. Megan's shoulders slumped with disappointment . . . and a bit of relief. "False alarm. It was just a parent."

"Okay," Sam said. "Stay up."

Just then, someone grunted so loudly into the airwaves that Megan flinched. The sudden sound was followed by a soft moan that soon shaped into words—words that raised a complaint about an injured "butt."

"Who was that?" Sam asked, his tone crisp and quick with concern.

It was Ella who provided the answer. "I'll give you a hint. He tells bad jokes and knows more about atomic matter than your average scientist."

Sam didn't need another clue. "Richie, you okay?"

❧ CHAPTER 30 ❧

THE MAN ON OLD COVE

Richie lay in a ditch, his glasses askew and his bag of candy spilled out beside him. He realized the sky was barely visible through the fog.

Sam's voice rose in his ear again: "Richie? You all right, man?"

"I . . . I fell." It was all Richie could think to say.

"How?"

Richie glanced toward the street, where a once-parked Radio Flyer wagon was now tipped on its side. "I tripped. On a wagon."

"Get up," Ella said curtly. "You didn't break anything."

"And how could you possibly know that?"

"Because I've seen you *not* break something a million times."

As Richie sat up, miniature candy bars and pixie sticks spilled down his chest. He stood and steadied himself. Then he freed his underwear from his rear end and continued down the street, his bag of candy now almost empty.

"Okay," Richie said. He straightened his glasses and adjusted his checkered nerd pants, pulling them high above his skinny stomach. "I'm on the move again."

"Roger," said Sam. "How does your street look?"

He scanned the houses. He couldn't see too far in the fog. "Everything looks good, I guess."

The airwaves fell silent. For the next fifteen minutes, the fog continued to thicken. It seemed to be slowly devouring the neighborhood, consuming houses and kids and cars. Porch lights struggled just to reach the street, and parents had begun to keep their children close. An intersection rose out of the fog and a street sign took shape. Richie had looped back around to Jenkins. He announced his position into his headset and headed down the road.

More time passed. Richie saw fewer kids trick-or-treating and porch lights were beginning to blink out. The other Crossers occasionally announced their positions—*"This is Noah. I'm headed onto Williams Road"* . . . *"Ella here. I just cut over to Phlox Drive"*—but mostly the airwaves stayed quiet.

As Richie paced down Jenkins Street, his eyes kept gravitating toward the Clarksville Zoo wall, which he could faintly see through the spaces between the houses. It looked eerie in the fog. Long and gray and winding, it had occasional cavities where large pieces of weathered concrete had crumbled away. Ivy clung to segments. Branches crept over its top like the hooked legs of giant spiders.

Realizing the streets were almost empty, Richie whispered, "Anyone know what time it is?"

"It's almost nine," someone said. Richie thought it had been Megan.

Solana spoke up. "Halloween's about over, then. At least by Clarksville's clock."

Richie veered onto another side street that continued straight for at least a hundred feet before curving back toward the Clarksville Zoo. As he came around the bend, he stopped so suddenly that his glasses jumped an inch down his nose. About thirty feet ahead of him, a man was headed in the same direction as Richie. He wore a hat with a wide, circular brim. And a trench coat—a long, flowing trench coat that stopped at his ankles.

Richie forced down a deep breath and said, "Guys . . . I have something here . . . a man . . . and he's dressed like DeGraff."

The airwaves stayed silent for a few seconds, then Noah's voice filled Richie's head. "Where are you?"

It took a moment for Richie to realize someone had spoken to him. He reached into his memory, discovered the question, and tried to remember where he was. Jenkins Street? No. Walkers Boulevard? Not there, either.

"Richie!"

"A side street. Ummm . . ." He turned his head and peered at a street sign until the words came into focus. "Old Cove—I'm on Old Cove."

"The man . . ." Sam said, "what *exactly* is he wearing?"

The man was beginning to sink into the fog, so Richie hurried forward a few steps. "A fedora hat. And a trench coat. I'm behind him—I can't see much."

"How tall?" someone said.

Richie couldn't think enough to answer.

"Richie—how tall!"

He concentrated. "Tall. More than six feet."

Silence claimed the airwaves. Finally, Sam said, "All right, everyone give me your positions."

One by one, the Crossers announced the streets they were on. Ella and Noah were just a few blocks over from Richie; Sam told them to get over to Old Cove.

"Richie," Sam said, "get closer to that guy, but don't let him spot you. Get a better look and let us know what you see—you got it?"

"Yeah," Richie said. "Get close."

Richie picked up his pace, the moist air curling around him as he moved in on the shadowy man.

~❧ CHAPTER 31 ❧~

ELLA RUNS FOR RICHIE

As Ella cut through the backyard of a white-bricked ranch, she trampled the remains of a vegetable garden and then hurdled the bottom half of a play structure slide. She cut between two houses, charged across their front lawns, and emerged on a new street, trying to build a mental image of her position in the neighborhood.

"Richie!" she said into her bone mic.

Richie's voice filled her head. "Yeah?"

"Where are you on Old Cove?"

"Huh?"

"The houses—what houses are you near?"

After a pause, Richie said, "Close to the Parkhills. And the house with the big boulder, the one painted blue."

She knew exactly where that was, about ten houses down, to her left.

"I'm coming," she said. Then she turned and took off running, her Wonder Woman cape waving behind her, her Lasso of Truth bouncing on her hip.

❦ CHAPTER 32 ❧

TANK AND THE TUNNEL

Tank swung his flashlight from spot to spot, revealing parts of the cave: the hard walls, the dirt floor, the passage leading to the Secret Zoo. As the fog headed for the outside air, it moved across his body like a living thing. It smelled of wet earth, and its weight filled his lungs. He occasionally waved his hands in front of him in a feeble attempt to sweep it away.

In his headset, he could hear the conversation between the scouts and Descenders. Tank thought to announce his position, then decided against it. Maybe it was safer to keep quiet for now.

The big man took a few more steps and then swept the beam of his flashlight up one wall, revealing an opening the size of a door. Tank had never seen it before. The passage was covered with a velvet curtain, moist air swirling and curling along its edges. Without a doubt, the fog was coming from here.

As he reached out and touched the gateway, magic surged up his arm. He eased the curtain to one side and peered around it. It was pitch-black. He took a deep breath and stepped forward, the velvet sliding across his shoulders and down his back, its magic delivering him into the Secret Zoo.

In his ear, the voices of the other Crossers immediately fell silent—radio waves couldn't span the magical divide between the two zoos. He raised the flashlight and lit the foggy air. He could faintly see that he'd stepped into another narrow cave, one that sloped down at a steep angle.

He took a step. Then another. He had to negotiate his movements with the slippery slope, his weight balanced back on his heels. The beam of his flashlight sliced through the fog, revealing very little. He noticed something about the walls. They were covered with narrow trenches that ran in all directions. He slid a finger through one trench; it was more than two inches across and easily as deep. He realized the tunnel had been dug out by hand—powerful hands with clawed fingertips.

"Sasquatches," he muttered.

He noticed something moving a few feet ahead and yanked his light in that direction. Something was crawling on the wall. A giant centipede. Easily the length of Tank's forearm, it had a dark body, yellow legs, and two pincerlike appendages curling out past its head. Its hard, segmented body curved like a snake, its dozens of legs pricking the moist dirt.

Tank turned to watch the centipede move past. He backed into a new spot and felt something soft and threadlike close on the skin of his bald head. He ducked low and aimed the light high. Cobwebs covered the ceiling, countless spiders scurrying across the silvery strands, their thin legs carrying plump bodies.

He swept his flashlight up and down the walls and noticed other insects: large ants and shiny beetles. They were undoubtedly coming from somewhere below—somewhere inside the Secret Zoo.

The big man took a nervous step and felt something crunch and pop beneath him. He swung his flashlight down at his boot and saw six spindly legs twitching in the gooey guts of an insect beneath it.

Realizing he should radio for backup, he decided to head back to the Clarksville Zoo. But with his first step, his feet slipped out from under him and he dropped to his back in the wet dirt. On the steep slope, he began to slide. Then, with a scream, he plummeted into the dark, foggy reaches of the hollow earth.

❧ CHAPTER 33 ❧

On to Old Cove

Ella peered through the fog as she ran up the street. Bright auras surrounded all points of light: flickering candlewicks, green glow sticks, the beams of flashlights. Porch bulbs looked like starbursts. She saw a few trick-or-treaters racing across lawns, their overstuffed bags swinging at their knees. Several houses down, she spotted the roof of the Parkhills' house.

Richie's voice suddenly rose in her head. "Guys, I'm close." Though he was surely whispering, his bone mic transmitted his voice loud and clear.

"How close?" Sam asked.

"Twenty feet, maybe."

"Can he see you?"

"No."

Ella cut into the yard next to the Parkhills' property. She ran as fast as she could. "Is he wearing boots, Richie? Black boots?"

Silence hit the airwaves, then: "Yeah."

Sam said, "Richie, don't get too close. This could be him."

"Wait a minute," Richie said. "He just stopped."

"Richie—does he see you?"

"He sees . . . something."

Silence followed. Ella reached the Parkhills' backyard and tore across it. Her heart was slamming in her chest, not from fatigue, but fear.

Richie said, "He just . . . he just turned around. Oh my . . . he's looking right at me!"

"Run!" Sam instructed. "Go! Get out of there!"

Richie screamed, and it was a barbaric sound, something produced from raw fear. His panic-filled voice filled the airwaves: *"Something's happening! My . . . my arms!"*

"Richie!" Ella called out.

A loud *thump!* erupted in Ella's earpiece, and she winced in pain. It was followed by silence.

"Richie!" Sam said, and Ella had never heard such urgency in his voice. *"Richie, come in!"*

Nothing. Richie was quiet.

"He dropped the bone mic!" a new voice said. Tameron. "His headpiece—it fell out!"

Ella ran alongside the Parkhills' house and charged into their front yard. As she did, Old Cove, the road Richie was on, began to rise out of the fog. She saw little else than occasional spots of light. But as she continued, a figure began to appear in the street. Then another. It was Richie, and a man whom Ella immediately identified as DeGraff. The Shadowist was off to one side of her friend, staggering about, his limbs flailing as he seemed to be struggling against something that Ella couldn't see. Richie was backpedaling away from DeGraff, screaming.

Ella gasped as she realized what was wrong with her friend. Parts of him . . . parts of him were *missing*.

CHAPTER 34

The Missing Pieces

Terrified, Richie had no clue what was happening. The man in the trench coat, DeGraff, had turned around—his face concealed between his collar and his hat brim—and spotted him. Then he'd charged, his gloved hands reaching out. But as he closed in on Richie, DeGraff's body was jolted to one side, and Richie simultaneously felt something strike his arms and chest. He looked down to see pieces of himself *gone*.

Now, Richie glanced over at his left arm. Though there was no blood or pain, he could see clear through to the ground. Gone were parts of his elbow, forearm, and all of his wrist. Had DeGraff spilled his wicked magic onto Richie's body?

His gaze jumped up to DeGraff. The man was off to one side of the road, staggering about and throwing wild punches into the air. But nothing was near him.

Richie groped at the missing piece of his wrist and touched something that wasn't part of his body—something that began to squirm. As he jerked his hand away, a visible piece of his forearm disappeared. It was as if some poisonous thing was moving along his arm, devouring his flesh. He grabbed the squirming thing, and it almost immediately appeared in his hand. A chameleon. Its buggy eyes were locked on Richie, and colors were swirling along its body as it tried to adjust to the new hues in Richie's palm. Within seconds, Richie's hand vanished in its perfect camouflage.

Richie suddenly realized what was happening. A Specter had attacked the Shadowist, and chameleons had fallen off her and landed on Richie.

As the chameleon climbed from his palm to his arm, Richie looked up at DeGraff, who was still struggling with the Specter, his long trench coat flapping against his boots.

"It's him!" Richie said into his bone mic. When no one responded, he realized his earpiece had fallen out. He spotted it on the ground, scooped it up, and plugged it back into its proper place. "Can you guys hear me?"

"Richie?" someone said. It had sounded like Noah.

"Guys, I—"

Before Richie could say more, someone ran up from out of the fog. Wonder Woman—Ella!

"Your arm!" Ella said.

"Chameleons!" Richie explained. "From a Specter!"

Just then, one of DeGraff's punches connected with the Specter, knocking a few chameleons into the air and revealing part of the girl: blond hair spiked in a Mohawk; bright blue eyes buried in dark makeup; smooth, pale skin. Sara.

The blow knocked Sara to the street. The chameleons that had fallen from her body scurried back onto her. DeGraff turned and ran.

"He's getting away!" Ella reported into her microphone. "Down Old Cove, toward Jenkins Street!"

"Roger," Sam said. "Everyone hear that? Converge on Jenkins Street and head him off before he can reach the zoo! Let's use this fog to *our* advantage!"

Ella turned to Richie. "You okay?"

Richie nodded.

"Sara?" Ella said, swinging her gaze around.

"Right here," Sara said, her voice rising directly from Richie's left. "I'm good."

"C'mon!" Ella said. "Let's go!"

Ella took off running. Richie followed, and as he brushed past Sara, the few chameleons on his body jumped back onto her.

Ella cast a glance over her shoulder. "Hurry, Richie! We can't lose him!"

Richie nodded and picked up speed. He'd never agreed with something more in his life.

ᴄᴇ CHAPTER 35 ᴈᴅ
Tank's Discovery

Tank slid down the steep cavern floor, his fingers slicing through the mud as he tried to grab onto something. Mud streamed up his pant legs, and his flashlight bounced around, streaking light across the walls.

When he came to a stop, a giant centipede crawled onto his neck, its body rubbing against his skin. He jumped to his feet and tossed the disgusting thing aside. Then he scanned his new position. The cave had leveled out. Less than five feet in front of him, it opened to a new area where nothing but fog and darkness waited.

He inched forward, the mud sloshing around his feet. He reached the mouth of the cave and stepped out. Then he swung the beam of his light along the wall near him and couldn't believe what he saw.

CHAPTER 36

DeGraff Pulls Away

Ella and Richie raced up Old Cove toward Jenkins Street. Ahead of them, DeGraff's black boots stomped the pavement and his trench coat waved like a cape. A woman pushing a toddler in a stroller suddenly appeared from the fog. She was dressed as a cat, her child a mouse. Startled by DeGraff, she yanked her stroller to the side of the road and yelled, "Slow Down!" without much kindness.

The scouts dodged left to avoid a kid dressed as Harry Potter, then rounded a curve in the road. Ella glanced over at Richie. Below his checkered flood pants, Ella saw at least six inches of stark white socks. Most of his shirt was buried in his pants, and the things in his pocket protector occasionally jumped out, leaving a trail of office supplies on the street.

DeGraff, faster than the scouts, began to pull away.

"We're losing him!" Ella said into her bone mic. "He's too fast!"

As they rounded a sharp turn in the road, DeGraff was gone, lost in the fog. Ella and Richie stopped. They didn't know if he'd continued down the street or charged into the surrounding lawns.

"He got away!" Ella said.

Sam's voice: "You sure?"

"Yeah." She braced her hands on her knees and swallowed a few deep breaths to cool the burn in her lungs. "He's gone."

After a few seconds of silence, Sam's voice rose again into Ella's ears: "Descenders—*find him*! Do whatever it takes!"

CHAPTER 37

HANNAH RUNS THE ROOF

Hannah turned off the street she was on and ran alongside a house. There were no trick-or-treaters in sight, and all the nearby porch lights were out. The darkness was as thick as the fog. She needed a better view, and she knew how to get it.

Still running, she jumped and tugged the pull-loops on her boots. Her rubbery soles bulged to ten inches thick. She shot upward, high above the houses, and landed on a gabled roof. Without breaking her stride, she hunched low to keep from being seen and ran across the shingles. At the end of the roof, she sailed easily across the distance to the next house, where she landed with a soft thud.

She looked right, then left. Through the fog, she detected the faint outlines of a few costume-clad kids. About ten rooftops in front of her, the row of houses stopped at Jenkins, the primary road through the subdivision, the one that wrapped around the Clarksville Zoo. On the other side of Jenkins were more houses, and beyond their backyards was the long concrete wall of the zoo.

Hannah sprang through the air again. If DeGraff was headed for the Clarksville Zoo, he would eventually have to cross Jenkins Street.

And Hannah hoped to be there waiting for him.

Solana Walks the Wall

Solana cut across several lawns and turned onto Jenkins. Not more than fifty feet ahead was Old Cove, where Ella and Richie had spotted DeGraff. She veered across the street, ran between two houses, and headed across a backyard to where the zoo wall stretched in both directions. She jumped, planted her palms on top of the wall, and pulled herself up. She quickly climbed to her feet and took off running. Though she couldn't see much through the fog, she could still see some activity in and out of the zoo. If she was lucky enough to spot DeGraff, she could move on him in an instant. She came to a stop in a place with a view between a pair of houses to Old Cove.

"I've got a good position," Solana announced into her bone mic. "I'm on the wall along Jenkins."

"Stay there," Sam spoke into her ear. "And be ready. Don't let this monster into our house."

"No way," Solana said. "That's not going to happen."

CHAPTER 39

TAMERON TAKES THE TOWER

At Clarksville Elementary, Tameron ran across the playground toward the back of the school. In the fog, the play equipment looked strange and eerie. Swings dangled like prison chains, and dome-shaped climbers sat like steel traps.

"I'm at the school." He spoke into his mic. "The Halloween party's over. The place looks empty."

"Stay put," Sam said. "Find a spot with a view."

Knowing what Sam meant, Tameron veered toward one of the wings of the school. As he ran, he pulled a strap on his large backpack. The canvas bottom dropped and released his tail. It uncoiled on the ground and dragged behind him, leaving a curling, snakelike trail in the wood chips. As he neared to within twenty feet of the building, he swung his tail high over his head, brought it down in a smooth arc, and catapulted himself onto the roof. He quickly retracted his tail and headed across the ceramic tiles.

On the peak of the main building, the Descender crouched beside the big bell tower, leaning his shoulder against one of its columns. He stared into the distance beyond the concrete courtyard in front of the school. Here, the fog wasn't so thick, and he could faintly make out several side streets and the winding stretch of Jenkins. The neighborhood was quiet and still.

"What time we got?" he asked.

"Nine-fifteen," Sam answered. "Streets should be empty by now."

This was good, Tameron thought. Get the people indoors, get them safe. Things were about to get very dangerous.

❧ CHAPTER 40 ❧

SAM SOARS INTO THE SKY

As Sam ran toward Jenkins Street, he said into his bone mic, "I'm going to find a spot between Old Cove and the school."

"You better hurry. . . ." Solana said into the airwaves.

"Why? What do we got?"

"Someone's coming down Old Cove. A man."

Sam uttered a curse. He stopped running. "Is it him?"

"I can't tell. He just cut into a corner lot. I can't . . . I can't see him now. It's too dark. And the fog . . ."

"Solana, tell me what—"

"Wait! He just turned onto Jenkins Street! He's headed

toward the school. He's about five blocks away from it."

"Don't lose sight of him." Sam paused, then said, "Hannah, what's your position?"

"I'm on the rooftops, headed toward the action."

Sam looked around, unsure. Then, he said, "Tameron— I'm coming your way."

"From which direction?" Tameron asked.

Sam considered this a moment, then said, "From above."

He retreated into the darkest recess he could find, a spot between two houses and a grouping of trees. He swatted his wrists against his hips, and with two loud clicks, the buckles on his jacket latched onto the zippers at the end of his sleeves. He raised his arms out to his sides, spreading the feathers from inside his jacket. Thin rods shot out from his cuffs, increasing his wingspan.

His transformation complete, Sam crouched low and sprang into the foggy air.

CHAPTER 41

THE CHASE

As Noah ran toward Jenkins Street, he was startled by a figure running out from a foggy yard. It was Megan, but Noah, having forgotten that his sister was dressed like a pirate, almost didn't recognize her. She turned and ran in his direction, joining him. Twenty feet ahead of the siblings, a man charged past on Jenkins Street—a man in a trench coat and a wide-brimmed hat.

"I've got Megan with me," Noah announced into the airwaves. "We spotted DeGraff on Jenkins, just past Pheasant Run."

"Follow him," Sam said. "Don't get too close."

"Roger," Noah said.

As Megan and Noah cut through a corner lot and headed after DeGraff, two figures rose out of the fog in a nearby yard—a screwy-looking kid with checkered flood pants and an oversized bow tie, and a girl with a gold headband, shiny steel bracelets, and a flowing cape. As they ran, the nerd tripped over his own feet and the young Wonder Woman leaped over a bush in superhero fashion. The two kids joined Noah and Megan on Jenkins Street, and together, the four scouts chased after the man the Secret Society desperately needed to keep out of the Secret Zoo.

CHAPTER 42

THE ENGRAVINGS

In the area that the tunnel had opened into, Tank stroked his flashlight beam along the wall. It was covered in slime and moss. Stringy green gunk dripped down its sides, and fog concealed its distant reaches. All along it were dark passages like the one he had just walked through. Caves. Caves that led to unknown places. Tank had never seen this part of the Secret Zoo—and it made him nervous.

Huge insects crawled across the walls. They moved in and out of the caves, their long bodies bending around curves.

Tank saw something above the mouth of the tunnel down which he'd slid: a deep engraving in the hard dirt. Letters. Peering forward, he read the word: "Rhinorama." This made perfect sense because Tank had just portaled into the Secret Zoo through the rhino exhibit in the Clarksville Zoo.

He moved the flashlight above a neighboring tunnel and noticed another deep engraving. Upon reading the words, he gasped and a jolt of terror surged across his body.

The engraving named a spot that wasn't associated with the Clarksville Zoo *or* the Secret Zoo.

The engraving read "Clarksville Elementary."

CHAPTER 43

THE DESCENDERS CLOSE IN

As Sam softly touched down on a rooftop, he closed his wings across his back and then dropped into the shadows of a wide chimney. The house faced Jenkins Street. To the right, about fifteen rooftops down, was Clarksville Elementary. In the fog, it looked odd and somehow threatening.

"Tameron . . . ," Sam said into his bone mic.

"Yeah."

"I can see Clarksville Elementary, but not you. What's your position?"

"Beside the bell tower."

Sam squinted to see through the fog. Though he made out the shape of the tower, he couldn't spot his friend. "How's the traffic down there?"

"There isn't any."

Just then, a figure came running up Jenkins Street. Fog whirled around a man in a trench coat and a fedora hat. Him.

"He's coming," Sam said. "Everyone up. Solana, you keeping a visual?"

"Roger," Solana said.

Crouched low, she was running along the five-inch cap of the concrete wall, the Clarksville Zoo to one side of her, the neighborhood to the other, as if she were rushing down the dividing line between two worlds.

Directly to her right was DeGraff, a row of houses and their lawns the only things dividing her from him. He moved in and out of Solana's view as trees, thick patches of fog, and other obstacles seemed to race past.

Solana said, "Who else has sight on the target?"

"I got him," Hannah said as she touched down on a new rooftop beside a chimney, smoke twining around her body. She dropped to her rear and pressed her back against the cold stack of bricks. Directly across Jenkins Street was Clarksville Elementary. Hannah peered at the foggy bell tower for Tameron, but couldn't see him.

"I'm across from the school," she said.

"By me?" Tameron asked.

"Yep."

"Give me a visual."

"See the two-story house blowing smoke?" Hannah asked.

"Yeah."

Hannah lifted her hand high and waved it in the streaming white vapor. "Hola."

"Perfect," said Sam. "We have him on all sides."

Hannah peered down Jenkins Street and watched the fog continue to break around DeGraff. "Sam," she said, "how you want to play this?"

"I'm working on it," Sam answered. He was still crouched low on the rooftop, his silver feathers blanketing the shingles around him. "Hannah—you seeing anyone in the street?"

"Negative."

"Tameron—anyone on your end yet?"

"Nope."

"Then I'm going to take him," Sam said.

"In the middle of the *street*?" Tameron asked.

"We can do this right now," Sam said. "We can *end* this."

Silence passed across the channel, then Ella's voice came on: "He's right. Let's bring this guy down. If we get spotted, so what; we'll deal with it."

Sam stood and scanned both ends of the street. Most of the porch lights were out. He charged down the rooftop, jumped over its edge, and snapped open his wings. After steering around a few tall trees, he coasted out above Jenkins Street.

As he passed over the scouts, DeGraff came into full view. He was running. About fifty feet in front of Sam, Clarksville Elementary rose from the fog.

One of Sam's wings whapped a branch, and DeGraff swung his shadowy face around. Seeing Sam, he lowered his head and picked up speed.

"He's headed for the west entrance of the zoo!" Tameron shouted into the airwaves.

"Sam!" Hannah shouted. *"Do it now!"*

Sam swept toward the street. With a thrust of his legs, four steel hooks sprang from each shoe. He sailed down, his talons aimed at DeGraff's shoulders. But just as Sam struck, DeGraff dove off the street and landed in a roll on the front lawn of Clarksville Elementary. Sam swung around in a wide circle, steering through the tall oaks along the curb and then crossing over Hannah. He saw DeGraff charge toward the school, away from the zoo wall.

"You guys seeing this?" Sam said.

After his friends answered yes, Solana asked, "What do you want us to do?"

"Descend," Sam instructed.

CHAPTER 44

THE FALL OF TANK

Tank stared at the engraving above the mouth of the tunnel: "Clarksville Elementary." Was it possible that this passage actually connected to the scouts' school? The thought filled him with dread.

A deep growl came from behind him, and before he could react, something struck the side of his head. He collapsed to the ground and lay there, pain pushing through his temples, light flashing across his sight. The ring in his ears was deafening. As the side of his face slowly sank into the mud, a large, spiny insect squirmed onto his neck, leaving a trail of slime. The world-gone-sideways began to blur as he teetered on the edge of consciousness.

Something moved into his vision. A foot—a foot the size of a child's torso. Mangy hair fell off its heel, sprouted between its toes, and dragged through the mud. Its nails were like swollen claws. A sasquatch.

Tank tried to move and couldn't. The world continued to gray, and the ringing became a low drone.

He heard a voice behind him—a deep, gravelly voice that seemed to come from something less than human: "Now bring me the others."

Something clutched Tank's ankles and hoisted his legs. A second later, he was being dragged backward. Mud oozed into his clothes and packed into his ear. Too stunned to resist, he watched a sasquatch move into the tunnel marked Clarksville Elementary, its shoulders slumped to fit beneath the low ceiling. The beast was followed by another, and another, and another. Before Tank could count their number, the drone in his ears stopped and the world went black.

❦ CHAPTER 45 ❦
THE CAPTURE

As Noah veered off Jenkins Street and led the scouts onto Clarksville Elementary's courtyard in pursuit of DeGraff, something appeared on the edges of his vision. He swung his head to see Solana running toward the school, her long, flat quills bouncing on her arms and torso and swinging from the backs of her hands. Just beyond her, Tameron dove from the school rooftop, thin bands of armor spreading across his body, his tail releasing from his canvas bag. As he landed, he lowered his shoulder and rolled on the ground, his armor protecting him. Then he ran after DeGraff, who had just charged off the courtyard and headed toward the back of the building.

Noah glanced at the other scouts. Ella's jaw hung open, Megan's lips moved with soundless words, and Richie's eyes seemed to swim behind his taped-up glasses. The three of them couldn't believe what was happening any more than Noah could.

As the four friends chased after DeGraff, Sam flew over them, the wind from his wings wagging Ella's cape and tossing Megan's pigtails. Hannah lunged from the peak of a nearby house and touched down briefly in the court-yard before springing up and out again. She passed over Sam and then touched down on top of the school's west wing.

DeGraff disappeared behind the corner of the building.

"Keep on him!" Sam said.

As Tameron and Solana rounded the corner, Sam swooped over the rooftop and Hannah jumped down to the other side. The scouts turned the corner after them and Noah watched as Hannah, in the air again, came down in front of DeGraff, who dodged left, then charged out into the playground. He only got a few feet before being blocked by Sam, who'd landed with his arms out to his sides, his wings open like a feathery wall. As DeGraff ran in a new direction, Solana plucked a hand-ful of quills and threw them. More than a dozen barbs studded DeGraff's backside. The Shadowist fell forward and tumbled through the wood chips. His hat fell off and rolled on its circular brim to a stop ten feet away.

The Descenders quickly surrounded him, and then so did the scouts. Facedown, DeGraff writhed in pain, quills sticking from his back and hamstrings like needle-thin daggers. Noah tried to see his face but could only make out a glimpse of his profile—his cheek, ear, and jawline. He looked human.

It was Sam who spoke first: "Get up."

No response. DeGraff continued to squirm, his sweeping limbs piling the wood chips at his sides. Around him stood the play equipment, its beams and bars looking like fresh frameworks of puny buildings.

Tameron kicked DeGraff's leg. "Get up before I make you get up."

The Shadowist said nothing. With his face still down, he reached around, grabbed a fistful of quills, and ripped them from his flesh. He howled in agony and tried to crawl away from the pain, his arms and legs slipping on the ground. After a few seconds, he stopped and lay there, his arms spread out in front of him, the soles of his black boots overturned. Then he did something that Noah doubted anyone would have imagined. He began to whimper. His broken cries were barely audible, but they were clear.

"*Get up!*" Tameron said. He reached down, seized a few of Solana's quills, and tore them from DeGraff's back. "*Up!*"

Noah grimaced as the Shadowist howled a second time. After a few seconds, his howl softened to a whimper.

"Guys," Noah said, "maybe we should—"

Tameron held up a finger at Noah—an unmistakable message for him to keep quiet. As Tameron reached down to grab more quills, Sam seized his wrist, stopping him.

"Hold up," Sam said.

Through the eyeholes in his thin helmet, Tameron stared at his friend.

Sam said nothing else. In his silence, DeGraff's sounds became louder, more distinct. DeGraff wasn't whimpering—he was *laughing*.

"You got to be kidding me," Tameron said. Then, to DeGraff: "What could you *possibly* be laughing at?"

His laughter grew louder and stronger. Then he slowly rolled over, the remaining quills in his back bending flat. As his face turned up, his full identity was revealed for the first time.

"This," he said. "I'm laughing at *this*."

Lying before them was a man the Crossers had seen before. He had a thin face and sunken cheeks covered in splotchy freckles. And even in the darkness and fog, the color of his hair was visible. Red.

"Charlie . . ." Noah breathed.

Charlie Red squinted his already-squinty eyes and bawled laughter. His breath wafted off his lips like smoke from the mouth of a dragon. The Crossers stood there, too stunned to speak.

Ella took a step forward. "Wait a minute—was it you in my front yard that night?"

A sudden peak in Charlie's wicked laughter confirmed that it was.

"But . . ." Megan said. "Why?"

After a few seconds, Charlie's laughter died down. "Why?" he said. He sat up to face Megan and winced at a fresh spot of pain along his back. "Why? Ohhh . . . you're about to see why."

A deafening crash erupted and everyone turned to see that the two rear doors of the lower-el wing of Clarksville Elementary had banged open, slamming into the brick wall of the school. One battered door dangled crookedly on its lower hinge. In the dark doorway, a beastly leg appeared, then an arm. Something was stepping out onto the playground. The creature had to crouch and turn its body sideways to fit through the frame. Then it moved out of the school.

"No," Sam uttered. "Impossible."

Standing just outside Clarksville Elementary was a sasquatch, its mangy hair dangling off its muscular limbs, its bottom fangs pinching its upper lip. It locked eyes on the Crossers and sliced its long claws through the misty air. The sasquatch was followed by another, and another, and another—more and more snaking their crouched bodies through the open doorway. In all, six appeared.

Charlie Red continued to laugh from the ground—a sound that was suddenly more haunting than any Noah had ever heard.

Charlie had led them into a trap.

The scouts huddled behind the Descenders, who lined up side by side to face their adversaries and prepared to fight.

From behind them rose Charlie's voice: "Now."

Noah swung his head back to see that Charlie wasn't speaking to the sasquatches—he was speaking into a walkie-talkie.

CHAPTER 46

THE ON POSITION

At the west zoo entrance, a security guard set down his walkie-talkie and rolled his chair over to a large black box beneath a table in the small shack. He opened its top, exposing rows of knobs, buttons, dials, and lights. A large red switch had two positions, *off* and *on*.

The guard gnawed on a toothpick, then rolled it across his lips. As he leaned over the box, a goopy bead of pus dripped onto it. He swiped it up with a fingertip and held it near his eyes. Then he touched the cut on the side of his face, the place from which the pus had fallen. The wound was moist, fresh; he felt its heat.

He smiled. His change was already happening, just as Charlie had promised.

He turned his attention back to the large box in front of him. It was an RF Jammer, a military-grade device that could block communications across different radio frequencies. Not long ago, Charlie had secretly delivered it to him.

The guard reached back into the case. With a twist and pull, he calibrated a few remaining settings. Then he turned the big red switch to the *on* position.

❧ CHAPTER 47 ☙

THE BATTLE ON THE PLAYGROUND

A loud pulsing sound erupted in Noah's ear. As he swung his hand up and turned off his headset, he realized the other Crossers were doing the same.

"We're being jammed!" Sam said. "The headsets—keep them off!"

Noah glanced behind him and watched the smile spread on Charlie's face. This was part of Charlie's plan.

The sasquatches crept forward, snarling, their bodies slinking in and out of the shifting fog. Streams of blood oozed from their infected gums and trickled off their lower lips.

Hannah stood braced to fight. Tameron swept his tail back and forth along the ground, spilling waves of wood chips across its spikes. Sam shook his wings and ruffled his feathers. Solana held clusters of quills in her fists.

Noah looked to his friends. Ella was pale with shock, and Richie's whole body was trembling. Even Megan was afraid, her eyes opened as far as the rims of her narrow glasses.

"Guys," Sam said, "we can't let these things leave the schoolyard. We do, and it's all over."

The Descenders nodded.

Sam swung his attention to the scouts. "I want you to get back. Get out of—"

Before he could finish, the sasquatches charged and the scouts bolted into the foggy playground, a strange landscape of steel bars and dangerous heights. The four friends quickly crouched behind a row of play panels with gears that spun, wheels that turned, and bells that rang. They peered over and around the panels, watching as the Descenders and sasquatches jumped at one another.

Solana released the quills from her grip. The barbs flew like miniature missiles and stuck into the front of a sasquatch, which grabbed and pulled at its chest, tearing them out. Solana plucked more quills from her jacket and attacked a second time.

"The sasquatches—how did they get into our *school*?" Megan asked.

With his gaze locked on the fight, Noah said, "I have no idea."

Tameron lunged forward and turned, sweeping around his tail about four feet off the ground. Two sasquatches dodged backward, just missing his attack, but a third wasn't so fortunate. It flew sideways and slammed down about ten feet away, plowing through wood chips and raising dust in the fog.

When a sasquatch cocked its arm to swipe at Sam, the Descender dove straight up. He kicked out his feet, released his talons, and clasped the sasquatch's arm as it passed beneath him. With a yank of his legs, he pulled the beast to the ground.

Hannah jumped onto her hands and flipped, planting her boots against the gut of a sasquatch. The beast buckled, shot backward through the air, and crashed against the brick wall of Clarksville Elementary, rattling the ceramic shingles on the rooftop.

To Noah, everything suddenly seemed impossible again. How could monsters live in a world connected to his? How could kids use magic to transform themselves? And how could these two groups be fighting on his school playground?

Tameron heaved his tail through the wood chips and

took out the legs of a sasquatch, which fell to its stomach with a ground-shaking thump. Hannah sprang forward, several stories high, and came down directly on its spine. The monster went limp, and its bloody tongue slipped from its mouth.

"Guys!" Ella said. She pointed over the panel in front of her, a tic-tac-toe game with large spinning letters. "Look!"

Over to one side was Charlie Red. A few quills still dangling from his back, he ran through the fracas and disappeared through the open doors of the school.

Megan jumped to her feet and swung around the panel in front of her. "We can't just let him get away!"

"Megan, wait!"

But Megan was already running after Charlie. She seemed to partly evaporate in the fog before disappearing in the dark school.

As Ella stood to chase after her best friend, Noah grabbed her arm and yanked her down beside him. The panel that she'd been hiding behind exploded into pieces, tic-tac-toe spinners shooting in all directions, bouncing and rolling across the playground. In the jagged remains of the panel stood a sasquatch, wood chips stuck in its hair. Its yellow eyes looked straight at Noah.

Noah peered around the sasquatch to Richie. "Go! Help Megan!"

Richie stood frozen in his nerd costume, his pants pulled high, his white socks exposed.

Ella waved her hand toward the school. *"Richie—go!"*

Richie turned and ran toward the dark doorway.

Ella and Noah had no choice but to turn and run the other way. They dodged a few play panels and headed across the playground. After a few seconds, they heard the sasquatch grunt and chase after them.

Ella cut across Noah, saying, "Follow me!"

She circled the merry-go-round and weaved through an assortment of spring riders—seats that were shaped like animals and rocked on giant springs. At the play structure, an elaborate contraption with slides and bridges and hutlike platforms, Ella jumped onto a short metal deck and bounded up the stairs. Noah followed. At the first hut, they huddled behind two plastic walls and hid from view.

They waited. They listened. They heard the now-distant sounds of the Descenders battling the sasquatches, but nothing else. With their knees pulled up to their chests and their arms wrapped around their shins, they were so close to each other that Noah could feel Ella's breath—warm and moist, like steam from a pot. Patches of dense fog rolled through the play structure, leaving wetness on their costumes. He thought of Megan and Richie and whatever danger they now faced in the school. He thought of the Descenders and how Sam had ordered the scouts away. Were the scouts useless? Had the Descenders been right a year ago to want them kept away?

They heard something. A grunt. Then a growl. The sasquatch was nearby. Something snapped loudly—a piece of metal, maybe. Noah peered out between two panels: the sasquatch had broken a spring, knocking a yellow duck to the ground. The beast took a few steps, grabbed a happy blue whale, and hurled it into the air. Noah pulled back his head. The sasquatch was coming their way.

Noah stared into Ella's eyes and mouthed, *Don't move.*

They soon heard another grunt, this one almost directly beneath them. Noah looked down. Through the openings in the metal grate, he saw the ground—a distant spread of wood chips.

Another sound came. A soft, rumbling growl, closer than ever. Through the grate, Noah saw nothing.

Then . . . something. A long leg of the sasquatch. Then its arm, its body.

The monster was directly beneath them.

❧ CHAPTER 48 ❧

THE PADLOCK

As Megan rushed deeper into the school, the sound of the fight faded and then vanished altogether. The only light in the lower-el wing of Clarksville Elementary streamed down from a pair of fluorescent bulbs toward the middle of the hall, leaving the ends dark. Megan peered into the distance and saw Charlie, his fedora hat once again on his head, his trench coat fluttering behind him. He turned right, disappearing from view.

She charged faster. Seconds later, she reached the end of the lower-el wing. The hallway continued straight, passing between the media center and the cafeteria. A new hallway branched off to her right.

Megan turned and chased after Charlie. To her left, the glass wall of the media center blurred past, a few lights revealing long rows of bookcases, tables, and computers. Megan sped past Halloween decor: fake cobwebs in corners, papier-mâché pumpkins in glass cabinets, black cat posters on the walls. She stopped at another corner and spotted Charlie Red nearing the far end of the hall.

"Charlie!"

Megan tore after him, lockers and classrooms streaming by. She passed through a cone of light and then closed in on Charlie, who'd stopped at the dead end. Two double doors blocked him from getting outside, a thick chain coiled around their steel handles. Charlie fumbled with the padlock, and Megan wondered why. Surely he didn't have a key—a security guard from the Clarksville Zoo had nothing to do with the school.

Then she realized what Charlie was doing. He was pulling down on the lock to make certain it was latched. Charlie wasn't trying to escape—he was making sure Megan couldn't.

She abruptly halted twenty feet from the end of the hall. "Charlie?"

Charlie turned and looked out at her from beneath the brim of his hat. He smiled a wicked smile and took a few steps toward her. Even in the dim light of the hallway,

Megan could see the spattering of oversized freckles across his face.

"Hey, Meg . . . funny we should meet here—the school, of all places."

She took a step back. Something was wrong with Charlie. He seemed . . . different. He had a new swagger in his walk, and a deep drawl in his voice, as if he was having trouble getting vowels out of his throat. As he took off his fedora hat and held it in his hands, his bangs dangled across his forehead. His hair seemed more red than ever before.

Megan collected her courage and spat out, "What are you doing?"

The corners of his mouth curled upward. "Me? I've simply embraced the inevitable."

Megan began to back up. She suddenly realized she didn't have a plan to stop Charlie. "What are you—? What's inevitable?"

Charlie moved toward her, his trench coat clapping against his feet. "Him."

"Who?" Megan asked. "DeGraff?"

Charlie nodded. "And it's very important now that you and your friends don't interfere."

A low growl sounded behind her and she spun around. At the far end of the hall, more than a hundred feet away, was a sasquatch. Like an ape, it was standing on its four limbs, rocking from side to side. When it threw back its head and roared, Megan saw the silhouette of its fangs. It dropped its chin and crept toward her.

Charlie walked past Megan and headed toward the far end of the hall. "Good-bye forever, Megan."

She simply stood still. Then she scanned her surroundings and fully realized her predicament.

She was totally trapped.

◄◙ CHAPTER 49 ◙►

THE SMELL OF FEAR

Richie, his eyes wide with fear, charged down the lower-el wing. Instead of following the first turn, as Megan had, he continued straight, running between the cafeteria and the media center. At a four-way intersection, he stopped. Ahead was the main entrance, its glass doors appearing as a small, clear rectangle. To his left and right were new hallways.

Richie turned his head one way, then the other. Which way was Megan?

He charged down the hallway to his right. He ran beside the long wall of the media center and then passed the hall that rejoined the lower-el wing. In the upper-el wing, he slowed down and scanned the classrooms as he moved through rows of lockers on both sides. He checked a few closed doors and discovered them locked. The hallway ended at an exit that was chained shut. There was no sign of Megan.

Richie started to return up the dimly lit hall and noticed something standing at the far end, beyond the main entrance and toward the gymnasium.

"Megan?" he muttered.

He peered forward and pulled the distant figure into focus. It was too big to be Megan. In fact, it was big enough to be only one thing. A sasquatch. Richie realized it was knuckle-walking, like an ape.

His heart dropped. He retreated a step and stared over his shoulder at the locked exit. There was no place for him to go.

The sasquatch moved to one side of the hall and began to sniff at something, a classroom door, perhaps. The sasquatch hadn't spotted Richie—at least Richie didn't think it had.

To get out of plain view, Richie dashed to the side of the hall and pressed his back against the lockers. When the metal doors clanked, he winced and stared up the hall, hoping he hadn't been heard. The sasquatch, now perfectly still, seemed to be looking in his direction.

He stretched himself flat against the lockers. Fear raised beads of sweat on his brow. With his chin on his shoulder, he continued to stare up the hall. For a long time, the sasquatch didn't move. Then it raised its snout and began to twitch its head. Richie realized it was pulling scents out of the air.

A drop of sweat streamed down Richie's temple. A second drop became trapped in his eyebrow. He'd once read that animals could smell fear. Had Richie given off an odor while running through the school?

The sasquatch suddenly looked down the upper-el wing of the school. Seconds slowly passed, and then the beast began to knuckle-walk toward Richie. It moved away from the gym and then past the main entrance, its pace slowly increasing.

Richie held his breath and kept perfectly still. He stared at the only intersection between him and the sasquatch, which was as far as a hundred feet away. He'd never be able to reach it in time.

The sasquatch began to heave its weight back and forth. And there was nothing Richie could do.

CHAPTER 50

THE CLUTCHES OF THE SASQUATCH

Ella realized that Noah was no longer breathing. Where she'd once felt his breath on her face, she now felt nothing at all.

The sasquatch was hunched directly beneath them. Through the steel grate, she saw the top of its head, the bulge of its back, and its hulkish shoulders. Its hair hung off its body, and its huge feet pressed wood chips into the ground. Silently, she began to will the monster away: *Move. Get out of here.*

The sasquatch took a step forward and stopped. Its upturned nose, shiny with snot, began to twitch as it sniffed the air.

Ella's stomach sank. The beast could smell them. Noah's eyes bulged, revealing that he understood this, too.

The sasquatch slowly craned its neck upward. Its crusty hair slid down its brow and off its swollen temples. It stared at the scouts, its yellow eyes streaked with blood-shot veins. Its fangs were as sharp and thick as the tusks of a boar. The thing beneath the scouts was no ani-mal—not anymore. Filled with the hate and magic of the Shadowist, it had evolved into a true monster.

The sasquatch threw up its fist and punched through the steel grate. It shoved its entire arm through and reached for the scouts. Noah rolled onto the bridge. The sasquatch swiped at Ella's leg and just missed, its open hand banging the metal grate and rocking the walls. Its huge fingers had square, knotty knuckles and were tipped with long claws.

As Ella tried to crawl away, the monster wrapped its powerful hand around her arm, just above her wrist.

❧ CHAPTER 51 ❧

A KEY TO SUCCESS

Within forty yards of Megan, the sasquatch passed into the bright light in the middle of the hall and was fully revealed: the wide wall of its teeth, the flex and release of its massive muscles.

In a panic, Megan ran to a classroom door, Room 203, Ms. Peter's class. The knob wouldn't turn. She ran to Room 205. It, too, was kept locked.

Barely more than forty lockers now separated the sasquatch from Megan. It passed Charlie Red, who casually walked on.

Megan dashed across the hall to Room 206 and cranked

the doorknob. Nothing. She seized the doorknob to Room 204, which was directly beside Room 206. Again, the knob wouldn't budge.

She stared up the hall again. Less than twenty lockers away, the sasquatch was now creeping forward on two feet, its arms raised. She saw the details of its face—its swollen lips, its black pupils, its dark nostrils. In seconds it would reach her . . . and it would kill her.

Megan's eyes moved to a poster above the lockers on the wall beside the sasquatch. On it was a picture of a closed book, the reader's spot marked with a gold key. A caption read, "Reading is your key to success."

Your *key.*

An idea sparked in her head. She unsnapped the small leather pouch on her pirate belt and pulled out the single item inside it, the gold key that Noah had dropped in the street. The *magical* gold key that could fit any lock in the Clarksville Zoo.

Could the key fit a lock *outside* the Clarksville Zoo?

She jabbed the key at the door. Expecting to hear the soft *clink* of the key jamming halfway into the lock, she instead heard nothing at all. The key had softened and sunk into the lock cylinder, just as it had for the doors in the Clarksville Zoo.

She turned the knob and pushed her way into the classroom. Just as the door slammed shut behind her, the sasquatch banged into it, rattling it inside its frame. The beast dropped its head and peered through the small window, its apelike nose pressed against the glass. Megan had a close-up view of its yellow eyes and square teeth.

She backed away and glanced around. This was Ms. Sara's third grade classroom. It had at least twenty individual desks in groups of four, and the walls were papered in drawings made of crayon. Normally Megan would have thought this room charming and fun, but now she thought of it as something else—a dead end, no better than the one in the hall.

The sasquatch pulled away from the door, leaving green, goopy snot on the glass. It disappeared from view.

"Leave," Megan muttered. "Please, please . . . just *leave*."

But right after her words, there was an enormous crash and the door snapped off its hinges and flew inward. It smashed into a group of desks and its window burst in a spray of glass. Two desks toppled over, spilling books and papers and crayons onto the floor. The sasquatch turned sideways and knuckle-walked through the open doorframe.

"No," Megan uttered.

Inside Room 204 of Clarksville Elementary, the sasquatch stood partially straight, pressing the mound of his back against the ceiling. Then it threw back its head and roared.

⚜ CHAPTER 52 ⚜

INSIDE LOCKER 518

Richie continued to stand with his back against the wall as the sasquatch advanced into the upper-el wing. Was Richie in plain view? He could only hope not.

He glanced around and saw the two walls of lockers stretching in both directions. Suddenly he had an idea.

He slid down to a nearby locker, where a thin metal plate read, "518." Richie's locker. He dialed in his combination and gently opened the door. Then he turned sideways, ducked his head to avoid the top shelf, and slipped inside, pulling the door closed behind him, but not allowing it to latch. His world went almost black. The only light came through the vent—five horizontal slits right in front of his face. Through them, he could see maybe fifty feet in either direction.

He waited. He listened. In the dark, confined space, he could hear his heart. Sweat streamed down his temples. His shallow breaths burst against the locker door and wafted back against his face.

He heard something. Footsteps. Then, in the edge of his vision, the sasquatch appeared. It stopped at the beginning of the upper-el wing and peered down the empty hall, its raised snout sniffing the air. It lowered its head, grunted, and scanned the rows of lockers.

Richie watched the beast knuckle-walk to the lockers along the opposite wall. It tipped its head to one side and seemed to wonder about them. It laid one palm flat against the door and softly pushed. The door buckled inward and snapped off its top hinge. Startled, the sasquatch jumped back and the door swung outward and dangled on its bottom hinge like a too-loose tooth ready for pulling. The sasquatch curiously sniffed the exposed space. Then it swung around and faced the hallway again. It swept its gaze down the lockers on one wall, then up the lockers on the other, still hunting for Richie's scent. It walked across the hall and back again. It seemed confused, and Richie realized why. Richie's scent was trapped in the locker, and the sasquatch couldn't pinpoint where he was.

The small space of Richie's locker was hotter than ever. Sweat had soaked the ribbed cuff of his cap and the armpits of his checkered nerd shirt. His breaths came in quiet, quick gasps.

The sasquatch suddenly lunged to one side and threw itself against the lockers, collapsing a few. Metal clanged and clunked, and fragments of steel burst into the air—latches and locks and small jagged pieces. Books and papers spilled out onto the floor. The monster kicked through the debris and took off toward Richie's side of the hall, disappearing from view before crashing into the lockers again. The exploding sounds rang in Richie's ears. Shreds of metal rained down on the hall floor, and pens and pencils rolled across the tiles.

Richie bit his bottom lip to keep from whimpering and tasted the salt of his sweat.

An animal grunt sounded, and then the sasquatch charged across the hall and slammed into several new lockers, smashing their doors and thin walls, emptying their guts onto the floor. It immediately ran to the other side and plowed into several more.

Its intentions became obvious.

The beast was going to move down the hall, crushing lockers until it crushed Richie.

CHAPTER 53

OVER THE BRIDGE

Pain shot from Ella's wrist to elbow. All the sasquatch needed to do was tighten its grip to crack and crumble her bones to pieces. Something grabbed her other arm, and she glanced over to see Noah holding her with two hands. He was leaning back on the bridge, trying to free her.

"*Ella—pull!*" he commanded.

Ella did as instructed, the web of pain spreading all the way to her shoulder. Just when she feared she'd never break loose, she fell away from the hut and tumbled over Noah onto the bridge. Stunned, she glanced back and saw the sasquatch holding the broken remains of her Wonder

Woman bracelet. The wide silver band had split in two and slipped off her arm, allowing her to pull free.

She turned to Noah, who said, "Defends against all manners of attack."

Ella nodded, too shocked for words.

Noah grabbed under her shoulder and pulled them both to their feet. "C'mon—we got to move!"

The scouts ran across the bridge, which had a metal grate for a floor and vertical rails for walls. The sasquatch, having freed its arm, jumped beneath them. It reached up and seized both sides of the grate. Then it dropped its weight to one side, snapping the brackets that connected the floor to the hut behind the scouts. The bridge tipped like a drawbridge as one end of it was forced down.

"Noah—hurry!"

Less than five feet separated the scouts from a new platform. The floor became a steeper and steeper incline as the sasquatch continued to pull. They were no longer simply crossing the bridge—they were *climbing* it.

As the scouts escaped onto the new platform, brackets and bolts snapped like gunshots and the bridge gave way and crashed to the ground. Tremors moved through the framework of the play structure.

"We have to make it back to the Descenders!" Noah said. "We'll never beat this thing on our own!"

A straight slide provided the quickest exit to the ground.

Three feet above the top of the slide ran a horizontal bar. Noah clutched it in both hands and flung his legs out in front of him, landing on his rear end on the slide. He touched down on the playground and took off running, his feet flinging wood chips into the air.

Ella followed. But as she released the horizontal bar, the sasquatch appeared at the side of the slide, its arm cocked back. It swung at her head, and Ella dropped down just in time to pass beneath the blow, which instantly buckled the slide, tipping up its bottom like a ramp. Ella coasted across the unexpected incline and flew several feet into the air, her arms and leg flailing. She hit the ground running and took off after Noah.

As the scouts dashed across the playground, Ella peered over her shoulder. The sasquatch had already dropped to its hands and feet and was rushing after them.

CHAPTER 54

AGAINST THE WHITEBOARD

Megan scanned the room for an escape. The outside wall had several windows, but they were surely kept locked, and Megan had no time to get them open. There were no doors other than the one she'd entered through. The only way out was the way she'd come in, and the sasquatch was blocking that passage. Having nowhere to go, she backed toward the front of the class.

The sasquatch crept toward her. It growled and snorted and dripped saliva off its bottom lip. When it bumped into one of the desks it had knocked over, it reached down, seized one of its metal legs, and casually hurled it aside. The spinning desk crashed into the ceiling and came down hard on the floor, breaking into several pieces.

Megan walked backward past several desks and stopped by the slick whiteboard on the front wall. To her right was Ms. Sara's desk. It was littered with books and paperwork and tins filled with assorted junk. A bunch of pens stood on end in a Mickey Mouse coffee mug, and yellow Post-It notes clung to everything: a lamp, a book, a box of tissues, a stapler.

The sasquatch cut across the room at an angle. Headed toward Megan, it plowed through the classroom furniture, its beefy arms heaving items everywhere. Chairs struck the walls, their plastic seats exploding to pieces. Desks flew and knocked over tables and shelves. Papers rained down like large confetti.

Unable to stay quiet any longer, Megan hollered, "Leave me alone!"

The sasquatch hurled another desk into the air, where it turned end over end, its open compartment spilling crayons and markers and pink erasers. The desk bounced off a filing cabinet and struck a window, leaving a web of cracks.

"DeGraff will *never* win!" Megan shouted. "Even if you kill me . . . it won't do any good!"

The sasquatch threw aside the last desk between it and

the front of the class and stepped up to Megan, looking bigger than ever.

"What are you going to do, huh?" Megan challenged. *"Kill a girl?"*

The monster answered by letting loose a roar so powerful that pain erupted in Megan's ears and the pens in Ms. Sara's Mickey Mouse cup shook.

CHAPTER 55

ALONG THE WALLS OF LOCKERS

The sasquatch crushed a group of lockers directly across from Richie. Handles and hinges tumbled through the air and clinked on the floor. The monster pulled itself from the crumpled remains and charged toward Richie, who watched from the slits in his locker vent. He shut his eyes and winced as the beast threw forward its weight. A deafening rattle stung his ears, and a second later Richie looked out to see the sasquatch charging back across the hall, leading with the mound of its muscular shoulder.

To Richie's right, the metal wall was now bulging inward—his locker had barely been missed.

The sasquatch continued to zigzag down the school, crushing lockers and dumping their contents onto the floor. When it reached the end of the wing, it turned and knuckle-walked back, its head swinging to survey the damage. Most of the lockers had been pulverized, but a few remained intact. The sasquatch again sniffed the air for Richie's smell.

Richie held his breath, his heart beating faster than ever. He realized he was drenched in sweat. If fear had a smell, he stank of it.

The sasquatch abruptly stopped in front of him and aimed its yellow-eyed gaze at his locker. It sniffed the air deeply, then swung its shoulders and knuckle-walked straight at him.

Richie's entire body clenched. A stream of sweat dripped off the tip of his nose.

The sasquatch leaned its head toward the locker vent. Richie watched its face come closer and closer. He began to smell its terrible scent, a cross between a wet dog and wet compost.

The beast pulled back its swollen, cracked lips, exposing the full length of its fangs. Then it leaned in so close that Richie could see nothing but the deep yellow of its eyes and the black of its pupils. The sasquatch was an inch or two away, and all that separated them was a flimsy steel door.

The sasquatch let out a low, rumbling growl.

Richie had been spotted.

CHAPTER 56

The Crawl Tube

Noah led Ella through the maze of playground equipment, her red cape fluttering behind her, the sasquatch charging after them on all fours. He veered right and headed for the school, which was still more than fifty yards away. Through the fog, the brawl began to take shape: Hannah leaping in the air; Sam flying overhead; Tameron heaving his tail. Hulking bodies lay on the ground. Sasquatches. It seemed the Descenders were winning.

Noah glanced back again. The sasquatch was only a few feet behind Ella. There was no way they were going to outrun it.

"Ella—follow me!"

"What the *heck* do you think I'm doing!"

Noah turned and dove into a plastic crawl tube, roughly fifteen feet long and four across. Each end was mounted on two poles which held it several feet in the air. A line of small oval cutouts, about three feet apart from one another, acted as windows. Ella dove in after Noah, and the two of them crawled to the middle of the tunnel.

The sasquatch slowed down and began to knuckle-walk beside the long piece of equipment, its stench wafting through the holes. Near the middle of the tube, it pressed its face against the plastic and peered inside, its angry yellow eye nearly filling the cutout. The scouts whimpered and pressed their backs against the far side of the tube. Ella kicked her flashy red boot against the cutout and the sasquatch grunted and pulled back. It hesitated, seemed to consider something, then knuckle-walked away, its furry muscles quaking as it grew smaller and smaller and then disappeared altogether in a cloud of dense fog.

The scouts, too stunned for words, sat there in silence. After a few seconds, Ella whispered, "Is it . . . gone?"

Noah shrugged. The two of them became very quiet again and listened.

The sasquatch suddenly appeared. On all fours, it was charging straight at them.

"Get down!" Noah said.

The scouts dropped in opposite directions, landing on their stomachs on the curved plastic floor. A second later the sasquatch punched its arm through a cutout and clawed at the open space, trying to grab one of the scouts as they squirmed away. Unable to reach them, it tried to pull free and couldn't—its arm was trapped. It roared and rocked its hulkish body back and forth, slamming against the crawl tube again and again.

Noah pointed to the open end of the tube beyond Ella. *"Go! Now's our chance!"*

As they clambered for the exit, the sasquatch thrust its full weight against the tube, knocking them off balance. The beast rammed the tube harder than ever. The circular walls began to quake. Then, all at once, the tube snapped off its posts and dropped several feet to the ground, the sasquatch's arm finally slipping free.

The sasquatch jumped to the end of the tube in front of Ella and lowered its overturned head into the opening. Its top lip drooped above its gum line, and drool dripped into its own eyes. In the small space of the tube, a growl rumbled like thunder. The sasquatch grabbed for the scouts, who screamed and crawled out of reach. The monster then pulled back its arm and knuckle-walked to the other end of the tunnel. As its face appeared in the opening, Ella and Noah retreated to their former spot toward the middle of the tube.

The sasquatch straightened its legs and hammered a fist down on the tunnel roof. The plastic cracked, and its blocky knuckles broke through. The beast tipped its head to one side and studied what it had done.

"Oh no," Ella said.

The sasquatch again knuckle-walked to the middle of the tube. It backed up about fifteen feet, charged forward, and slammed into the plastic wall, which buckled inward as the tube went into a roll. The scouts thrashed, their bodies turning along the revolving curve of the floor. The tunnel wheeled about fifteen feet and came to a stop.

Noah untangled himself and touched the spot that the sasquatch had struck. Along the plastic was a web of cracks.

"He's going to rip this thing apart," he said. "To get to us."

Ella crawled out from under her cape, which had settled on top of her head. "How far is the school?"

Noah glanced through one of the cutouts and saw the foggy images of the Descenders.

"Fifty yards," Noah said. "Maybe more."

"We have to make a run for it," Ella said.

As she turned for the exit, Noah seized her shoulder. "Wait."

"Wait for *what*?"

In response, Noah stood on his knees, gripped the

edges of two cutouts on the side opposite the sasquatch, and pulled down. The tunnel wheeled forward about a foot and stopped.

"We can move this thing," Noah said. "It'll keep us safe."

The sasquatch struck the tube again, sending it into another roll. Noah and Ella were tossed about until the tube came to a stop, ten feet away from its previous spot. The scouts got to their knees and once more faced the wall opposite the sasquatch. They reached over their heads, gripped the edges of two cutouts, and pulled down while heaving their weight forward. As the tunnel began to turn, they walked their arms along the wall. The tube rolled faster, the scouts crawling along inside it like hamsters in a wheel.

Noah peered through a cutout over his shoulder just in time to see the sasquatch bearing down on them again.

"Hold on!"

Their heads rocked and they shot forward as the sasquatch hit. The tube rose slightly off the ground and then bounced as it landed, throwing Noah and Ella off balance. They quickly stabilized themselves and kept crawling along the spinning wall.

"Go! Go!" Noah said.

As they rolled forward, playground equipment zipped past: a spiral slide, a freestanding rock wall, a swinging gate. Noah peered out through the cutouts and spotted the Descenders standing side by side. They were less than twenty-five yards away now, the defeated sasquatches lying all around them.

The sasquatch rammed into the tube, which went airborne again. As the tunnel touched down, it took off with more speed than ever. Noah felt the web of fractures beneath his fingers. It was growing, branching in new directions.

Ella and Noah were moving in near-perfect unison now. As they closed to within fifteen yards of the Descenders, the sasquatch delivered another blow to the crawl tube, which split in two and veered off in opposite directions, Ella in one half and Noah in the other. Ella's tube rolled to a halt by Sam, Noah's by Solana. The four teenagers spun to face the sasquatch, who skidded to a stop in front of them, wood chips piling onto its big feet.

With a smirk, Sam said, "Hi there."

Hannah sprang into the air and delivered a kick to the monster's chin, dropping it to the ground, where it shuddered once and then lay perfectly still.

Solana squatted beside Ella's tube and peered inside. She nodded and stroked her fingertips along the plastic curve. "Inventive, I'll give you that."

Ella crawled out and staggered to her feet. Her gold headband was turned sideways and her Lasso of Truth was coiled around one of her boots. As she rearranged her wardrobe, she stuck out her tongue at Solana in a way that was only half playful.

The Crossers turned to the open doors. This wasn't over. Charlie Red had to be stopped. His capture would surely lead the Secret Society to DeGraff. And Megan and Richie were alone in the school.

Sam took off running toward the building and the group followed. One by one, they passed through the open doorway into the dark and dangerous halls of Clarksville Elementary.

⚜ CHAPTER 57 ⚜

AVAST, YE SCALLYWAG!

The sasquatch raised its arm to strike at Megan, who covered her head with her arms and turned sideways in a feeble effort to protect herself. As she did, she felt something tug at her waist, and her pirate sword dropped to the ground and bounced a few times like a stiff fish out of water. The sasquatch gave a quick, nervous grunt and took a small step back.

Megan saw a chance, however minuscule. She snatched up the sword and thrust the plastic point of its blade directly between the eyes of the sasquatch. The monster gave another startled grunt and pulled back its head a few inches.

"Avast, ye scallywag!" Megan said, the words finding their own way onto her tongue. The long sword trembled in her unsteady hand.

The sasquatch let out a slow, rumbling growl, its gaze shifting from Megan to the sword. Its nostrils twitched as it sniffed the air in front of the fake blade. It suddenly seemed uncertain about everything.

Megan thrust the sword forward, causing the sasquatch to jump aside and crumple the frame of a fallen desk. She stepped into the space she'd opened and steered herself around the front of Ms. Sara's desk, positioning the distant classroom door behind her. The sasquatch turned as well, its gaze bouncing from Megan to the tip of the sword, which continued to hover inches in front of its face.

A hint of hope raised the volume of Megan's voice: "*Avast!* Stay away you . . . you *filthy thing!*"

The sasquatch clenched its fists, growled, but did nothing else. It believed in the danger of her sword.

Megan retreated toward the door, carefully maneuvering around twisted steel and shards of laminate desktops. She stepped over books and notepads and half-empty boxes of colored pencils. The sasquatch followed, crushing anything in its path. As it realized where she was headed, it flexed its outstretched arms and roared, raining spit all around. Megan tightened her grip on the sword and wagged its tip at the sasquatch.

"Don't!" she cautioned as she steered her way through the debris. "Just keep away!"

She crossed the remainder of the room, walking backward the whole time. As she moved through the doorway into the dimly lit hall, the sasquatch did, too. She turned toward the distant media center and headed that way. The sasquatch followed, its hunched back dragging along the ceiling.

Her rearward steps found a rhythm, and she moved more quickly, the sasquatch growing more and more irritated. At the end of the hall, the beast cocked its arms and seemed ready to lunge forward. Megan stopped it by swinging her sword in a long arc. The sasquatch dropped back on its huge heels. Megan again wagged the plastic blade, threatening more. She stepped into the two-story hallway in front of the media center. The sasquatch tried to circle her, but she kept it at bay by following its movements with the point of her sword.

By the time Megan neared the lower-el wing, the sasquatch couldn't contain its rage any longer. It swung at Megan, who instinctively ducked. Though the blow missed her, it struck her sword. The sasquatch pulled back its arm with a nervous snort and examined it. When it realized it wasn't injured—that Megan's sword wasn't a real weapon—it grabbed the plastic blade out of her grasp and cast it aside.

As Megan turned to run, the sasquatch seized the calf of her leg. Then, for Megan, Clarksville Elementary was overturned as she was lifted feetfirst into the air.

CHAPTER 58

The Steel Confines of Locker 518

Richie stared through the vent at the shadowy eyes of the sasquatch. At any moment the beast might crush him. Richie had to do something—but what? He was trapped in the steel confines of his locker with nothing but his books and his half-empty pocket of nerd-gear.

An idea struck him. His nerd-gear . . .

He fumbled through his shirt pocket and plucked out his squirt pen. He aimed the barrel at a slit in the vent and pressed the spring-loaded push-button, and ink streamed into the sasquatch's eyes. As the beast roared and reached for its face, Richie pushed open the locker, slamming the door against the monster's forehead. He crouched low, squirmed through the sasquatch's legs, and bolted across the hall, where he slipped into one of the few undamaged lockers and silently eased the door shut. In the new darkness, he stared out through the vent.

The sasquatch swiped at its face and staggered about. It shook its head and tried to blink away the ink. Then it stared into locker 518 and realized Richie was gone. Roars of anger rocked the hallway, and the sasquatch charged up the upper-el wing, undoubtedly thinking Richie had gone that way. Richie lost sight of it through the locker vent, and a moment later he heard a deafening clang of metal. Silence followed. Then footsteps. Someone or something was headed toward him. The sasquatch? Charlie Red? In a panic, he aimed his squirt pen at the vent. The footsteps grew louder and louder. Then a shadowy figure filled Richie's view. The locker door sprang open, and Richie sent a spray of ink into the air. The ink didn't connect with a sasquatch or Charlie Red, because standing in front of him was Ella.

Richie eased back his thumb and the stream of ink slowly went limp and then stopped altogether. "Oops."

Ella stared down at the fresh stain on her dress, her jaw hanging open. After a long, silent moment, she said, "Are you freaking kidding me?"

"I thought you were a sasquatch!" Richie explained.

Ella's eyes grew wider. "Dressed as *Wonder Woman*?"

"I . . . I freaked out. I'm sorry!"

Ella seized Richie by his oversized collar and yanked him into the hall. "C'mon, doofus! You spend enough time in the lockers during the week."

As they charged up the hall, Richie saw what had happened to the sasquatch—the Descenders. Standing at the end of the upper-el wing were Sam, Hannah, and Solana. Noah was there, too. The sasquatch lay in a heap beside a row of dented lockers.

"Where's Megan?" Richie asked.

"Don't worry," Ella said as they joined the other Crossers. "Tameron's got it covered."

CHAPTER 59

MEGAN AND THE SASQUATCH

Megan dangled upside down in the air, her head near the knees of the sasquatch. Out of nowhere, something suddenly coiled around the monster's waist. What looked like the body of a huge snake, Megan realized, was a tail—Tameron's tail.

The tail seemed to shrink on itself as it cinched tighter and tighter. The sasquatch dropped Megan and grabbed and punched at the thing around its waist. Its monstrous body began to bulge in strange places. Within seconds, it spasmed, jerked, and abruptly went limp. The tail uncoiled and the beast slipped to the floor, where it lay dead, its spine undoubtedly broken. Then the tail slunk away from the scene and gathered in its normal position behind Tameron.

Tameron stepped forward and offered his hand to Megan, who seized it and was hauled to her feet. She forced herself to look away from the dead sasquatch, hoping she'd eventually forget the gruesome way its life had ended.

"Where are the others?" she asked.

Tameron didn't need to respond because the other Crossers charged up to them from the upper-el wing. As they approached, Sam said, "Everyone all right?"

The two of them nodded.

"Anyone seen Charlie?" Tameron asked.

Heads shook.

"C'mon," Sam said. "He's here somewhere. Let's get him before he *isn't*."

Sam led the Crossers along the glass wall of the media center and swung around a corner. Near the middle of the long hall was a room marked, "Maintenance and Electrical." Its door was wide open.

"Charlie?" Hannah asked.

They shared a curious look, then Sam said, "One way to find out."

Together, they crept into the maintenance room.

CHAPTER 60

THE CELLAR

The maintenance room was the size of a classroom and crowded with large appliances that hummed and sputtered and spat. Pipes stretched across the open space, connecting steel boxes, disappearing into the walls, and passing through valves with large red handles. One appliance had so many pipes jutting from it that Noah was reminded of a spider.

There was no sign of Charlie. But the back of the room had a large door—and it was open.

Sam turned to the scouts. "You know where that goes?"

The scouts shook their heads.

Sam considered the door for a moment, then said, "C'mon" as he moved toward it, his wings sweeping along the equipment. The other Crossers followed, Tameron's long tail stroking the floor like the sinuous body of a huge snake.

At the open door, Sam bent down to pick up something. He showed it to the others: a broken padlock. This door was normally kept locked. As the Crossers moved closer, they were met with a cool draft of air. They peered over one another's shoulders. A steep flight of dusty concrete steps led to a dirt floor. A cellar—an *old* one.

Richie said, "This has got to be from the old school— the one they demolished."

The other scouts nodded in agreement.

Sam pointed down. In the ground several feet from the bottom step was a faint impression of a large foot with hooked claws. A sasquatch had been here. But the toe prints were facing the steps, as if the sasquatch had walked out from the cellar rather than in.

Sam headed down the stairs, waving his hand for the others to follow. As Noah stepped down, the underground air overwhelmed him. The decades-old smell of must and earth seemed to have a weight. Directly off the staircase was a long hall, roughly six feet across and a hundred feet long. Both of the uneven concrete walls had four carved-out sections for doors. The hall was dimly lit by a few bulbs that dangled overhead in simple fixtures. Dust had settled across everything: the lights, the floor, the pebbly concrete.

With soft and cautious footsteps, Sam led the slow charge into the hall. None of the Crossers dared to speak. A sasquatch had been here—how and why, no one knew. Were there others? And what about Charlie Red?

Sam peered through the doorway into the first room on his left. He looked around and then glanced backed at the Crossers. With a nod, he led everyone deeper down the hall. As Noah passed the room, he looked inside to see an old furnace covered in a layer of dirt. Pipes reached out from its large steel body and punched through the ceiling like the arms of a robotic octopus.

The dirt floor absorbed the sounds of their footfalls. Other than the drone of the appliances back in the maintenance room, the world had fallen eerily silent.

Sam peered into the doorway to his right. Empty. He led the group farther and stared into a new doorway. Again, nothing, and the group pressed on.

Roughly fifty feet away, a figure strolled out from a room near the end of the hall, and the Crossers froze. The figure casually turned and faced their group, the dim light revealing Charlie Red.

Sam said, "Red—it's over."

Charlie chuckled. "I hardly think so."

"Look around," Solana said. "There's eight of us and one of you. And we got you against the wall."

Charlie looked into the dark shadows behind him. "A dead end?"

"That's right," Sam said.

"How can you be sure?"

The Crossers said nothing.

After a few seconds, Charlie continued, "Before you charge down and . . . *apprehend* me . . . can I offer some help with something?"

Sam looked puzzled. He said nothing.

"Would you like your radios working again?"

"You jammed them? How—?"

"You underestimate me," Charlie said. He unclipped a walkie-talkie from his hip and raised it to his lips. "Please give the airwaves back to our friends. Over."

Sam said, "Who are you talking to? Who else is in on—"

"Go ahead and try," Charlie said.

"Huh?"

"Your headsets—try them now."

Everyone reached to their ears and turned the headsets on. The pulsing sound was gone.

"Nice," Charlie said. "Now . . . you're probably going to want to radio in a request."

"A *what*?"

Charlie chuckled. He didn't speak for what seemed a long time. At last, he said, "How far are you willing to go to keep the secrets of your precious zoo safe?"

The Crossers stayed silent and waited for more. Noah felt his heart beating way too fast.

"You got quite a mess upstairs," Charlie said. "It's going to be real tough to cover up. That kind of damage—what will you blame it on? Humans can't do that. But some animals . . . some animals *can*."

Noah's stomach sank as he realized what Charlie was getting at. He wanted Sam to radio back to the Secret Society and have them release some animals into Clarksville Elementary. Gifteds, for certain—animals that could respond to commands from people and move easily into action. And animals large enough to cause destruction like this.

"No!" Noah said. He jumped forward and grabbed Sam's arm. "Don't!"

Charlie lifted the walkie-talkie to his lips and radioed his unknown contact a second time. "Can you also call our friends at the Clarksville Police? It seems there's been a terrible break-in at the school."

Sam became very quiet and very still. Then he glanced over at Tameron, who reluctantly nodded at him, a scowl on his mostly masked face. Into his bone mic, Sam said, "Anyone out there?"

Noah squeezed Sam's arm. *"No!"*

The Descender shrugged off Noah's hand. "It has to be done."

Noah glanced down the hall and watched the smile spread on Charlie's face.

A voice filled the radio waves. "Jay here. You back online? I was starting to think—"

"Jay, I need you to send two of our biggest animals to the school. Gifteds."

"What for?"

"We got a mess. And we need to clean it up."

There was a pause from Jay as he seemed to realize what Sam was getting at. Sam wasn't just looking for assistance—he was looking for sacrifices.

"Who do you want?"

Sam stared at the ground and shook his head in what seemed to be regret and disgust. "Blizzard and Little Big."

"Sam—no!" This time it was Ella. "The police—*they'll kill them!*"

Noah understood this might be the best way to keep the Secret Zoo safe, but every piece of his heart told him it was the wrong call. Blizzard and Little Bighorn were his friends, not pawns in a chess match.

After a few seconds, Jay said, "Sam . . . you sure we can't—"

"Send them!" Sam said. "And do it quick! The cops are already on their way!"

Hearing this, Charlie Red smiled, his freckles seeming to squirm across his cheeks.

Ella stepped forward and jabbed her finger at Charlie. "You knew this was going to happen! You *wanted* the sasquatches to smash up the school!"

"Well . . . that much is obvious, I think. But aren't you curious about why we're standing here"—he gestured toward the walls—"in this filthy cellar?"

The Crossers said nothing. Noah saw that Sam's feathers had begun to tremble.

"I *brought* you here," Charlie said. "For him."

Noah suddenly realized something. Charlie was no longer wearing the outfit that looked like DeGraff's. He had on his usual security guard uniform.

"Guys . . ." Noah said, his tone heavy with concern. "Where is—?"

Before Noah could get his question out, he had his answer. A tall man emerged from the same door Charlie had come through. He wore a fedora hat and a flowing trench coat.

DeGraff. The Shadowist. For real, this time.

Sam took a step forward and raised his arms out to the height of his waist, shielding the other Crossers with a wall of silver feathers.

DeGraff found a spot beside Charlie. He stared up the hall, his face cloaked in the shadow of his wide-brimmed hat. His trench coat, draped around his feet, was as dark and featureless as the shadows around him. He wore black, pointed-toe boots and sleek leather gloves. His arms dangled at his sides, and his hands were closed into fists.

For a long time, no one said a word. The two groups simply faced off from opposite ends of the long hallway. The overhead bulbs cast cones of light along the walls and floor. Richie stared out with wide eyes through his oversized glasses. Ella hid behind Solana, peering around the Descender's quill-covered arm. Megan stood sideways, looking poised to jump in any direction. Noah felt something strike his heels, and he looked down to see Tameron's tail twining through the Crossers' feet.

"DeGraff," Sam said at last. "That is your real name, isn't it?"

For a long time it seemed the man wouldn't answer. Then his hat bobbed up and down in a *yes* response.

"What do you want?" Sam said.

After a long pause, DeGraff spoke for the first time: "Everything." His voice gurgled out, as if his throat was coated in phlegm. He sounded human, but barely alive. He slowly lifted his arm and pointed a gloved finger at Sam. "But I'll start with you."

The Shadowist suddenly jumped forward and swung his arm over his head with unexpected agility. His hand struck a dangling fixture and sent it into a wild swing. Beams of light carved through the darkness. He took several long strides and smacked a second fixture, which reeled in all directions, casting light across the walls, the floor, the ceiling.

What happened next was impossible. DeGraff disappeared. One second he was there, and the next he was not.

"Where is he?" Tameron shouted.

Noah quickly recalled the stories he'd heard of Jonathan DeGraff, the legends and the half-truths. It was said he could walk into the shadows, move among them, *become* them.

The bulbs continued to swing around and around, striping the walls with light. The shadows in the hallway seemed to come alive.

Noah wondered if they had.

There was a muffled scream, and then one of Sam's wings swept across the group. DeGraff had appeared behind Sam, his hand covering the teenager's mouth. The Shadowist had something in his grasp—a piece of velvet, like that in the curtains and the Descenders' clothes.

Sam struggled for a second, then his expression fell flat, his body limp. Whatever was in the cloth—a chemical? the magic itself?—had rendered him unconscious. Sam toppled over, his wings dusting the walls. His head bounced on the dirt floor, and an instant later DeGraff grabbed his arms and dragged him toward Charlie Red, flashes of light revealing the horrifying scene in fragments, like a movie with frames missing. As the two of them moved into a shadow, they vanished and immediately appeared in the dim light at the end of the hall. It was as if they'd fallen into the darkness—as if DeGraff had taken Sam there. Then DeGraff dragged the Descender's limp body through the open doorway that he and Charlie had stepped through. It all happened so quickly—two, maybe three seconds.

The fixtures continued to swing, making it feel as though a flash of lightning had somehow become trapped in the narrow cavity of the hall.

Hannah was the first to react, screaming out Sam's name and charging up the hallway. After a few steps, her body swung violently to one side and she banged into the wall. DeGraff was behind her, his hand pressed to her face, the piece of velvet covering her nose and mouth. Hannah struggled for a few seconds. Then her body went limp, and DeGraff seized her wrists and the two of them disappeared into the darkness left by a flash of light. A second later she was being dragged into the same room as Sam. Charlie stood at the end of the hall, smiling. Then he turned and walked into the room—his work was done here; DeGraff would manage the rest.

Tameron looked at Solana. *"The scouts—get them out of here!"*

Solana didn't hesitate. She grabbed Megan's and Ella's shoulders, spun them around, and pushed them toward the exit, yelling *"Go!"* in a half-trembling voice. Richie followed. As Solana yanked Noah ahead of herself, Noah's gaze landed on one wall and he realized bugs were climbing on it—big bugs, the kind from distant lands. He saw plump-bodied spiders, giant cockroaches, and spiny-legged things with shiny shells. At first Noah had no idea where they were coming from, but then he figured it out.

Him. DeGraff. Somehow the Shadowist was leaving a trail of bugs. If was as if the insects were falling out of his body.

As the scouts headed for the exit, Noah heard a struggle behind him and realized Tameron was being taken down. He glanced over his shoulder to see the Descender's enormous tail sweeping through the air and banging against the walls. Then it dropped to the ground and lay there like the tail of a dead dinosaur.

Noah ran—he ran as fast as he ever had. He chased the scouts across the cellar and up the stairs to the maintenance room. But as he reached the top step, he heard a muffled cry behind him and glanced over his shoulder again. DeGraff had moved in behind Solana and was now pressing his velvet to her face. The Descender was staring straight ahead, her eyes bulging with terror. With one arm extended and fingers splayed, she was reaching for help.

Noah stopped. It took only a second for DeGraff to choke the consciousness out of his friend. Her knees buckled, and her body dropped to the hard ground. Dozens of her quills were embedded in the front of DeGraff, but they didn't seem to hurt him. Noah didn't know what was protecting DeGraff, his leather jacket or his magic.

Noah turned toward his friends, but they'd already charged out of the maintenance room and into the school hall. He swung his head back. Solana still lay on the ground, her long hair spilled out around her, her lips coated in dirt. As DeGraff hoisted her legs and began to drag her down the hall by her ankles, pictures of Solana flashed in Noah's mind; he saw her standing in Metr-APE-olis on their first encounter, walking through Koala Kastle, and sitting so close to him on the bench in the Forest of Flight. Something ignited in his chest and his entire body flushed with heat—a heat which burned away all fear. A second later he felt the soles of his feet pounding the steps, and then he was running up the hall after Solana. A swinging shadow passed over DeGraff and he stepped twenty feet through it into the light at the end of the hall, dragging his captive.

"No!" Noah heard himself yell. But his words weren't really coming from him—they were coming from a place *inside* of him, a place full of unspent emotions and untold secrets—a place full of power.

As DeGraff dragged Solana into the room where he'd taken the others, Noah charged across the cellar, adrenaline coursing through his body. He raced past the first room, the second, the third, insects bursting beneath his feet. At the end of the hall, he turned into the room. Small, it had concrete walls, a dirt floor, and pipes along the ceiling. DeGraff was headed to a place along the far side, the sight of which stopped Noah in his tracks.

The outside wall had a hole big enough to fit two side-by-side adults. On the floor was a dusty pile of rubble—jagged concrete pieces that had once been a part of the wall. Bunched to one side of the opening was a velvet curtain, the kind used in the portals of the Secret Zoo. Beyond it, a dark tunnel descended steeply into the ground, tree roots and clumps of earth dangling from its walls and ceiling.

The Shadowist stopped at the mouth of the tunnel. He turned his head—and what Noah saw terrified him. DeGraff didn't have a nose, just two holes in his face. The better part of his chin was missing. His top lip and the flesh above it were gone, exposing a black gum line and rotten teeth. The rest of his face was still intact, except for a wide tear along his cheek that exposed a strip of white bone. His skin looked rubbery and strange, as if it weren't skin at all, but an elastic material wrapped around his head, something to keep his flesh from spilling out. Noah remembered something Sam had once said: "Others say DeGraff is part shadow and part human—rotting flesh held together by the shadows' magic." DeGraff had been alive over a hundred years; what remained of his body was barely more than a corpse. The only part of DeGraff that Noah couldn't see were his eyes; beneath the brim of his fedora hat, they stayed hidden.

DeGraff tipped his head to one side to size up Noah. As he did, a large centipede crawled out from the gash in his cheek and disappeared into the collar of his trench coat. He reached up and casually scratched the skin below the wound, as if the centipede's legs had tickled. The skin along the bottom of his mouth curled upward, and Noah realized in a sickening way that DeGraff was smiling. The Shadowist made a deep, guttural sound almost like a croak and then started to step backward into the tunnel, dragging his captive along.

Just as Solana was about to be pulled into the tunnel, Noah felt his feet moving again and he realized he was charging straight at the hole in the wall. In the edges of his vision, the room blurred, and just before he would have trampled Solana, he dove into the air with so much force that it felt like he was flying. He plowed his shoulder into DeGraff's gut, buckling him and freeing Solana from his grasp. The two of them crashed down the steep tunnel and went into a roll, DeGraff's knees and elbows knocking against Noah, and the flaps of his open jacket slapping Noah's face. As Noah came to a stop about ten feet from the mouth of the tunnel, he spun onto his back and stared across his body to see DeGraff farther below. About fifty feet behind DeGraff, a sasquatch was dragging Tameron into the black, hidden depths.

Bugs, by the hundreds, were swarming on the dirt walls—spiders and beetles and other unnamable things. Only once had Noah seen so many insects—in the Secret Creepy Critters when he and Podgy had brought down the portal to Gator Falls.

DeGraff lifted his head to stare at Noah. His fedora hat was still in place, still masking his eyes. Noah could see that the two holes where his nose should have been were now packed with dirt. And spiders were pouring out of the wound in his cheek and skittering across his face, some disappearing beneath the flaps of his loose flesh.

With his insides churning with revulsion, Noah spun over onto his stomach and began to crawl up the steep incline, his feet occasionally slipping in the dirt. He glanced back to see that DeGraff was following. Just as Noah clapped down one hand on the hard dirt floor of the cellar, he felt something squeeze his left ankle, and he realized DeGraff had him in his clutches. Noah's fingers slipped through the dirt as he was pulled down. He turned onto his back and thought of the Descenders— Sam, Hannah, and Tameron. What fate waited for them at the end of this tunnel? Whatever it was, it wasn't going to be Noah's or Solana's.

He hoisted his right knee all the way up to his chest and then brought it down with all the strength he had. The sole of his boot landed squarely on DeGraff's cheek, whose head rocked back as his hat tumbled off. As DeGraff put both hands to his injured face, Noah dove through the mouth of the tunnel and landed beside Solana. He knew what he needed to do next—in the tunnel beneath Gator Falls, he'd seen what happened to a gateway once it was stripped of its magic curtain.

Noah got to his knees. As he reached up for the curtain, he caught sight of DeGraff again. The gash in his cheek was larger, and his face was dotted with the guts of spiders. He had short, unruly hair with bald patches, and his eyes . . . his eyes were *gone*. What remained were two black sockets as dark as the skull cavities of his nose. The Shadowist sprang off his knees toward the mouth of the tunnel and Noah yanked on the curtain, pulling it free from its rod. As more than a dozen gold rings clinked down on the floor, the chunks of concrete around Noah began to shift and shake. Then, all at once, they jumped into the air and fit into their previous spots in the wall, like pieces of a puzzle. They closed the hole and sealed its cracks. DeGraff and the portal were gone.

Noah leaned over Solana, calling her name. He lightly shook her shoulders. "Wake up!"

When she didn't respond, he slapped her cheek, hard. Solana closed her open mouth and then pursed her lips when she felt the dirt on them. She scrunched up her face and slowly opened her eyes to peer at Noah.

Three figures appeared at the door—Noah's friends, their eyes full of fright. They charged into the room and dropped down to their knees by Solana.

"We got halfway down the hall and realized you weren't with us," Megan said. "What happened?"

Noah ignored his sister and kept his attention on Solana, saying, "You okay?"

Solana shifted her gaze and took in the room. Her eyes quickly filled with awareness and life, and she propped herself up on her elbows. "Wha—?" she said. "DeGraff . . ."

"Gone." Noah lifted one end of the curtain toward Solana and said, "A portal." He helped her to a seated position. "You okay?" he asked again.

Solana nodded as she rubbed her eyes.

"Portal?" Richie asked. "How—"

Noah shook his head. "I don't know."

A noise suddenly invaded the room from above—a shrill, pulsating wail muffled by dirt and concrete. It was the sound of sirens—*police* sirens.

Noah raised his gaze toward the ceiling. "Blizzard and Little Big . . ." he said. "No . . ."

He hooked his arm under Solana's and, with Ella's help, hoisted her up. Solana swayed on her feet and then quickly found her balance. "C'mon—we got to go," Noah urged.

As he headed for the door, Solana stopped him, saying, "Wait!"

"Huh?"

She pointed to the curtain on the floor.

"Oh." Noah turned back and balled the curtain up under his arm. "Right."

He led the charge out of the room and down the hall, where the gooey remains of dead bugs were spread along the floor like spatterings of paint. As he went, he kept glancing over his shoulder to ensure Solana was stable on her feet—Ella was still helping her a bit.

As Noah made his way up the stairs, he said, "C'mon, we got to help Blizzard and Little Big."

"No!" Solana said.

Noah stopped and peered back. Solana now looked as

strong as she ever had, and Noah guessed the effects of the velvet had already worn off.

"We can't. You have to let them go. It's part of what they're willing to do—it's part of what they *want* to do."

But Noah would not stand by while Blizzard and Little Bighorn were made sacrifices.

"It's not what *I* want to do," he said.

And he charged the rest of the way up the stairs, the rest of the group following.

❧ CHAPTER 61 ☙

THE FALL OF FRIENDS

Outside the maintenance room, Noah headed down the hall between the media center and the cafeteria, Solana quietly calling out twice for him to stop. In the dark distance, he saw two police officers charge across an intersecting hallway and head left, their voices and footfalls quickly fading.

"Where are they going?" Richie asked from just behind him.

As they reached the new hall seconds later, Noah pointed to the floor, where two faint sets of dusty animal footprints headed in the same direction the officers had gone. One had three stubby toes; the other had five round toe prints and a wide sole. Little Bighorn and Blizzard, no doubt. As Noah turned to follow them, he saw the two officers bang through the double doors of the gym. Through the walls came the muffled sounds of people yelling and footfalls thumping on bleachers. And Noah heard something else. Animals—animals growling and grunting.

Noah slowed down at the gym entrance and eased open one of the double doors.

"Noah!" Solana said. "We can't—"

Before she could finish, Noah slipped through the crack.

Near the stage at the far side of the gym were Blizzard and Little Bighorn. They were backed against each other, their rumps almost touching. As many as a dozen officers were posted along the two sets of bleachers, their guns aimed at the animals. They were hollering questions and commands at one another, spewing profanities that echoed in the open gym. A man with a faint mustache was struggling to steady his gun. A woman was repeatedly shouting, "Animal Control—Where's Animal Control?" into a walkie-talkie. A hulking man was holding his stare down the barrel of a rifle while saying, "I got the shot! I got the shot!" and asking if he should take it.

Blizzard, his back arched high, was snarling and swinging his long neck from side to side. Against the brown basketball court, his fur was startlingly white. Little Bighorn had his head dropped low and his huge horn raised like a weapon. His unblinking eyes kept shifting around the room.

The officers crept along the bleachers toward the stage. They walked behind their weapons. Blizzard and Little Bighorn were in their sights.

Solana and the other scouts had slipped into the gym and joined Noah. Beside the bleachers, they were mostly hidden from view. Ella said, "What do we do?"

Solana, her Descender gear back inside her clothes, said, "Nothing. The animals are doing what needs to be done." She seized Ella's arm and pulled her back. "C'mon, we got to go. You want to spend the night in a cop station? Besides . . ." Her voice trailed off. Then she turned to her trapped animal friends and finished her thought. "We don't want to see this."

Ella yanked her arm away. "We can't just leave them!"

"We don't have—"

A voice rang out over the noise: "Bobby, take the shot!"

"Roger," said the brawny officer. He set his face against the rifle, his fat cheek bulging over the stock. Noah saw how his neck was nearly as thick as his head, rigid with muscles and corded with veins.

The other officers ceased all movement and conversation. Other than the low, rumbling growl of Blizzard and the occasional snort of Little Bighorn, the room had fallen deathly quiet.

A deafening crack erupted. As the brawny officer's body rocked, so did Blizzard's. The bear swung around, howling in pain. In his white fur, a bright red spot appeared. Just behind the shoulder of his right front leg, Blizzard had been shot.

The cop steadied his shaky rifle, his fat cheek again ballooning over the wooden handle.

Blizzard swung toward the officer. In any other circumstance, he would have charged up the bleachers and fought back. But not this time. This time he was doing what he'd come to do. To stand and protect his precious Secret Zoo.

A second blast sounded and Blizzard's body rocked again. As the gunshot echoed in the gym, Blizzard lowered himself to the ground, and a dull expression of acceptance found his face.

Little Bighorn turned to his fallen friend. The rhinoceros knew what was happening—he understood that the officer would eventually turn the rifle on him.

Noah heard whimpering and turned toward his friends. All the scouts were standing in shock, tears streaming down from their eyes. Ella had turned away, her hands pressed over her face.

Solana grabbed Megan's and Richie's elbows.

"C'mon—we got to get out of here!"

The brawny cop readied himself for a third shot. As he did, Noah pulled away from his friends, dropped the velvet curtain from his arms, and charged across the floor, screaming, *"No!"*

The cop fired but, having been startled, missed his target and instead struck the stage, splinters of wood showering into the air. As Noah ran across the court, all heads swung toward him. One officer yelled, and another screamed profanities. Before they could react, Noah reached Blizzard and dropped to his knees and began to frantically stroke the bear's head.

"You're going to be okay—everything's going to be okay." But even as Noah said the words, he knew how ridiculous they sounded. Nothing was going to be okay.

Blizzard turned his eyes to Noah. Countless emotions stirred in their dark depths. Then they settled, leaving Blizzard with one state. Peace. Noah could see what it meant for Blizzard to have him near—the boy he had shared so many adventures with in the past year. If Blizzard was going to die, he was going to do so bathed in Noah's love.

"It's okay," Noah said as his hand worked back and forth. "I'm here—I'm with you."

Noah felt something under his armpits, and his world blurred as he was pulled into the air. Inches from his ear, a voice erupted: *"His legs! Get his legs!"* An officer jumped in front of him and swept up his feet. The two men broke into a sideways jog and carried him off, Blizzard watching.

Noah screamed in anger as the two officers rushed him away. In the bleachers, the man with the rifle raised his weapon again. Seeing this, Noah yelled to be let go. He twisted and squirmed and kicked. It was no use; the officers were too strong.

A safe distance away from Blizzard, the officers dropped Noah, who immediately turned back to the stage and saw something that took his breath. Ella, Megan, and Richie were standing where Noah had just been. They were holding hands, their bodies as far apart as their arms would allow. Tears were still streaming down their faces. Just past their ankles lay the big white mound of Blizzard. The officers weren't going to put another bullet in their friend—not without putting one through them first.

Blizzard lifted his chin off the court and sniffed the air toward the three friends, taking in whatever scents came with their courage and love.

The officers erupted in panic. Feet pounded down the bleachers and everyone converged on the scene, their guns held in front of them. Rubbery soles squeaked along the floor.

The scouts didn't move. They stood their ground in

front of Blizzard, their hands clasped, their chests out. Noah saw that their tears had stopped. Their fear and sorrow had been wiped out by something else. Purpose.

Noah rolled onto his knees and then stood like his friends. Goose bumps rose on his arms. Blizzard and Little Bighorn had come to do something—but so had the scouts.

The stage curtain suddenly parted and out stepped two men. One had a rifle, but neither was dressed in the same blue uniform as the police officers.

As the cops dragged Noah's friends away, the man on the stage with the rifle fired a shot at Blizzard. The resulting *crack!* wasn't nearly as loud as the others, and as a bright green spot appeared in Blizzard's fur, Noah understood why. The rifle had fired a dart. The new weapon was a tranquilizer gun. The men on stage weren't police officers; they were officers from Animal Control.

A second dart was fired, then a third. Blizzard struggled to his feet, lumbered a few steps, and then his legs gave out. He lay on the basketball court, his front legs twisted beneath his body, his rear ones sprawled out. His eyelids sank half closed and his jaw dropped limply to one side as sedatives coursed through his body. He wasn't unconscious, but he was on his way.

Then the man fired several consecutive darts into Little Bighorn. The rhino stepped, staggered, and then collapsed to his stomach. His enormous head slumped, and his vacant stare fell to the floor.

One of the Animal Control officers hollered, "Everyone out! Lock the doors! We got a confined space here—let's use it! It's going to take a while for these animals to fall asleep!"

Officers quickly made for the double doors, holstering their guns along the way. Several officers seized the scouts' arms and pulled them along. As Noah went, he peered back to see Blizzard's side rising up and down with long, slow breaths. The bear turned his head, their eyes briefly met, then Noah was pulled out into the hall.

The officers released the scouts. Noah hugged his sister and saw that Ella was crying again. He looked for Solana and realized she was gone. She must have slipped out during the commotion, hopefully undetected. He peered back into the gym and saw that the curtain was gone— Solana must have taken it.

The final officer stepped into the hall. He unholstered his billy club and jammed it through the handles on the double doors, securing them. Noah was horrified at the thought of Blizzard being barricaded in the room. What would Animal Control do with him? What would happen to Little Bighorn?

The officers, more than a dozen, turned to the scouts. The cop that had fired at Blizzard reached out and grabbed a handful of Noah's shirt and one of Richie's. "Are you out of your minds? I could've killed you in there!"

Two officers intervened, pulling their coworker away from the kids.

"You were shooting him!" Megan said. "You were going to kill him!"

"He was following orders!" another officer spoke up. Noah turned to the voice and saw a man with tidy hair and a neatly trimmed mustache. His uniform seemed freshly pressed. To Noah, it looked like he was in charge. The man turned to the other officers and said, "Check the halls and the classrooms. Look for other animals or injured civilians." The officers broke down the hall and split in different directions, their footfalls quickly fading.

The man turned to the scouts and said, "I'm Officer Jones."

The scouts, huddled close, nodded.

"You kids mind telling me what the *heck* you're doing in here?" Officer Jones asked, his tone crisp and curt.

"We heard the noise," Megan said before her friends could respond. "We were walking by"—she pinched the fabric on her pirate uniform and held it toward the officer—"trick-or-treating. When we saw the commotion at the school, all the cop cars and stuff, we came inside." She paused before adding, "It was probably a dumb thing to do, but this is our neighborhood. We were just concerned."

Officer Jones stared at Megan. Then he slowly looked at the other scouts, who were nodding in agreement. He lifted a single eyebrow and seemed to consider Megan's story.

"Is anyone hurt?"

The scouts shook their heads.

"And what about you, kid?" The man pointed to Noah. "That bear do anything to you?"

"I'm fine," Noah said.

"Yeah, well . . . you came pretty close to getting your heads chewed off. That bear could have—"

Just then, an officer came charging back up the hall. Seeing the frantic look on his face, Jones said, "What's wrong?"

"TV's here!"

Officer Jones threw back his head and muttered something under his breath.

Ella turned to Richie and mouthed, *TV?*

"Reporters," Richie whispered.

Jones waved the man away, saying, "Go! Keep them off the property!"

The officer turned and ran.

Jones turned back to the scouts and said, "No one else?"

"Huh?" said Noah.

"Just the four of you, right? No one else with you?"

"Un-uh," Noah said. "Just us. We were trick-or-treating and—"

"Yeah, yeah . . . I got that already." He became quiet for what seemed a long time. In the silence, Noah could hear faint footsteps as officers searched the halls. "You didn't see anything I should know about?"

They shook their heads.

He seemed to consider something. Then he pulled a small notebook from his jacket pocket, flipped it open, and readied his pen on the page. "Give me your names and addresses." Once they did, Jones stuffed the notebook back into his pocket and waved them off. "Go—get out of here. I got too much to worry about right now. I know how to find you if I need to."

The scouts turned to leave. But after only a few steps, Noah swung back, saying, "Sir?" He looked toward the double doors of the gym, where the police baton was wedged between the handles. "The animals . . . are they going to be okay?"

"The bear . . . he took a few bullets—you saw that. And Animal Control . . . it's difficult to know what they'll do. We can't have animals running through the neighborhood, kid. People could get hurt."

Noah stared at the door a moment longer—it was the closest he could get to seeing his friends. After a few seconds, he said, "People already did."

Noah watched confusion twist the officer's face. Then he turned and left without another word.

The scouts headed down the hall. They pushed through the main entrance and walked out onto the concrete courtyard to an assault of bright lights, noise, and commotion. At least fifteen police cars were parked around, their roof-mounted light bars flashing red and blue across everything: the grass, the school, even the cops themselves. Several cars had their door-mounted spotlights turned toward the main entrance—bright streams in the still-foggy air. In the street, a crowd was gathered: mothers and fathers, and kids dressed in costumes, some carrying bags full of candy.

The scouts left the scene and headed down Jenkins Street. Noah, staring straight ahead, declared, "We won't let them die." He paused, then added, "None of them. Blizzard, Little Big, the Descenders . . . we'll get them all back."

It wasn't just a remark—it was a vow. And on the dark, foggy street, the other scouts nodded and pledged the same.

❧ CHAPTER 62 ☙
Keeping Secrets

When police officers discovered a classroom and two rows of student lockers in ruins, they assumed that Blizzard and Little Bighorn had caused the damage. Had they investigated the school minutes before, they would have learned the truth.

During the confrontation in the gym, a group of six girls had arrived at Clarksville Elementary. They divided into pairs to search the school. Their intent was simple: to discover the bodies of the sasquatches and bury them in the secrecy and magic that literally crawled along the girls.

In the upper-el wing; Evie and Sara found a sasquatch

lying on the floor, its long, limp tongue dangling over its slack jaw. As they rushed toward it, they each held open one of their pockets, releasing chameleons from the Portal Place in the Secret Zoo. Hundreds spilled out across the floor and crawled onto the sasquatch, squirming through its mangy fur. Within seconds, the beast seemed to disappear.

In front of the media center, Lee-Lee and Elakshi discovered the body of a second sasquatch and did the same.

Both pairs of Specters then went to work on getting the sasquatches out of Clarksville Elementary. For this, they relied on the chameleons again. Using their massive numbers, the chameleons could lift things many times their size. Countless chameleons squirmed beneath each sasquatch, taking its incredible weight onto their backs. Then they carried each beast in secrecy through the halls and out the broken doors of the lower-el wing.

Outside, the Specters led the chameleons across the foggy stretch of the playground. They secretly crossed Jenkins Street and headed toward the gates on the west side of the zoo. Once behind the cover of the concrete wall, the Specters appeared and flagged down several guards to take over the sasquatches. As the girls rushed back to Clarksville Elementary, the chameleons swarmed up their legs and vanished back through the portals in their pockets.

All six Specters met up on the playground, where six fallen sasquatches lay. They opened their pockets and quickly went to work. The chameleons lifted the sasquatches again and followed the Specters in perfect secrecy across the playground and to the zoo. Then, their work done, the chameleons crawled back into the Specter's pockets, and Evie and her friends fully appeared. Without a word, the six girls turned and headed deeper into the zoo.

Near Metr-APE-olis, a voice called out to them: "Evie, wait!"

Across the zoo grounds, Solana came running. She stopped in front of Evie, took a deep breath, and asked, "How did you know?" When Evie's only response was a blank expression, she added, "How did you know to come to the school?"

Evie considered the question. Then she reached into one ear and plucked out a bone mic. She tossed it to Solana, who instinctively caught it. Solana looked at the mic for a second and then held it out to Evie. "Here," she said. "You should keep it."

Evie crossed her arms.

With her hand still reaching out, Solana said, "Things can be different. We can make this work again."

All the Specters but Evie looked away.

Solana said, "DeGraff—he captured my friends. Sam,

Tameron, Hannah—he got them all. Maybe . . . maybe you could help."

Seconds passed. Evie started to say something and stopped. Then she turned and walked off, leading her group deeper into the zoo and leaving Solana with the bone mic in her hand.

Solana stood and watched her go. She glanced at the headset. Then she called out, "Evie, hold up!" and charged after the girls.

Hearing Solana, the Specters opened their pockets and invited the chameleons to crawl along their bodies again. Then the six girls escaped Solana by escaping the world.

❧ CHAPTER 63 ❧

THE CONSTRUCTOR

As the Specters disposed of the sasquatches, an officer named David Banks entered a room beside the school cafeteria marked "Maintenance and Electrical." As he searched with his gun drawn, he noticed an open door and peered through it to see a short flight of steps leading down to an old cellar. Grotesque insects were crawling on the concrete walls: bulbous beetles, thick-legged spiders, and long, slinky centipedes.

He glanced over his shoulder and then softly closed the door. As he realized there was no way to lock it, he saw something on the ground. A broken padlock. He picked it up and turned it over in his hand. The U-shaped shackle had been ripped from its steel body.

He heard footsteps. Another officer was approaching. He quickly fed the broken shackle through the hasp on the door. Then he reached into his jacket, pulled out a small, velvet cloth, and wrapped it around the square piece of steel. He waited a moment and felt his fingers tingle.

"Banks?"

He turned, a bit too abruptly. Standing at the doorway was a fellow officer, Jimmy Thornton. Banks slipped the velvet back into his jacket pocket, hoping Jimmy hadn't noticed.

"Yeah?" Banks said.

"Everything okay in here?"

Banks nodded. "Room's clear."

Jimmy looked once at Banks's hand, which was now empty. Then he nodded and headed down the hall.

Officer Banks extracted the velvet and wrapped the padlock in it a second time. Once again, the magic of the Secret Zoo went to work.

David Banks—a man who had a wife, three children, and a house and had spent more than fifteen years working for the Clarksville Police—was more than an officer. Like the scouts, he was a Crosser. But he also served the Secret Society as a Constructor, a person specialized in repairing damages to the Clarksville Zoo and its surrounding areas. Sometimes the tools were ordinary. Other times they were not.

Officer Banks silently counted to fifteen and pulled away the velvet. The lock was fully repaired. He stuffed the material into his pocket, turned, and fled the room, certain he had more work to do.

⚜ CHAPTER 64 ⚜

An Old Acquaintance

On the streets of the City of Species, Mr. Darby stepped up to the main entrance of the Secret Creepy Critters. From the outside, the sector resembled the main Clarksville Zoo exhibit to which it was attached. Its core building had walls that rose in the air like those of an ancient castle, supporting a dome-shaped roof. Dozens of wings projected in all directions like the jointed limbs of a giant spider. Sick-green moss spread like a disease over the building's stone blocks.

It was storming in the city. Dark clouds had made dusk of day. Rain fell sideways, pounding the streets and the buildings. Streams poured over sidewalks, and puddles covered everything. Most of the animals had retreated into the sectors.

Mr. Darby stopped twenty feet in front of the portal into the Secret Creepy Critters. The gateway was being guarded by two Descenders. They were in gear: one had spikes along her shoulders and back; the other had long, elephant-like tusks reaching out from the sleeves of his leather jacket.

Standing with his wet gray hair and beard clinging to his body, Mr. Darby uttered, "Leave me."

The Descenders quickly nodded and rushed off.

Two curtains came together at the middle of the gateway. In the hard wind, the heavy velvet rolled and waved. The curtains occasionally flapped apart, revealing the darkness kept captive within the sector walls.

Mr. Darby suddenly called out, "*DeGraff!*"

The old man stared at the portal and waited. Rainwater beaded on his dark sunglasses. Wind shaped the curtains in new ways.

"*DeGraff!*" Mr. Darby called out, louder this time.

For a few minutes, nothing happened. Then the rain-soaked velvet began to bulge as something from inside pressed against it.

Was it him? Was it the man that had haunted and hunted the Secret Zoo for nearly a century?

The hump in the curtain began to take shape. The thing pushing against it walked on four legs. An animal. Or something like an animal, anyway.

Something appeared through the slit between the curtains. A brown snout. Next appeared a large, round head covered in fur, and then a massive brown body. Through the opening stepped a huge grizzly bear.

Or what had once been a grizzly anyway.

Mr. Darby instinctively took a step back. Then he forced himself to stand his ground. Through the rain-streaked air, the thing-that-had-once-been-a-bear stalked toward him, its paws splashing through puddles. Twice the size of an average bear, its fur was matted and muddy, and patches had fallen out, exposing black skin. Its over-sized claws gouged the concrete. It walked with its head low, the wide mound of its back high. The bear blinked and then met Mr. Darby's gaze, revealing eyes that were colored red.

In front of Mr. Darby was an animal that had been poisoned by DeGraff. Mr. Darby knew this because he'd seen the sasquatches change in the same way.

The bear stopped and rolled its head in a small circle. Mr. Darby noticed something that made his stomach churn. Insects were squirming and crawling through the bear's fur—spiders and beetles and worms.

The bear opened its jaws and a wet wad of paper

tumbled out. Mr. Darby looked at the wrinkled lump for a moment and then snatched it off the street. He unwadded it and read:

I'm back, old friend.

The small statement sent a chill of terror through Mr. Darby. The thing-that-had-once-been-a-bear turned, walked across the street, and disappeared back into the Secret Creepy Critters, the curtains swaying in its wake.

Mr. Darby stared toward the portal in silence. Memories filled his head. He clenched his hand around the paper and dropped the crumpled ball to the street, where a gust of wind sent it tumbling away.

"You won't destroy me," Mr. Darby muttered to the empty space between him and the sector where DeGraff was hidden. "Not a second time."

The old man stood there a moment longer, his dark sunglasses concealing his eyes, his wet velvet jacket clinging to his shoulders and back. Then he sharply turned and walked off, his boots splashing mud across the once-colorful streets of the City of Species, which was now a city under attack.

READ ON FOR A SNEAK PREVIEW OF
THE SCOUTS' CONTINUING ADVENTURES!

❧ PRELUDE ❧

THE CAPTIVES

DeGraff, the Shadowist, backed away from the portal to the City of Species, something of a smile on what remained of his face. He turned and moved deeper into the Creepy Critters sector of the Secret Zoo, the thing-that-had-once-been-a-bear walking beside him. Seconds ago, the animal had delivered a note to Mr. Darby—a note with a very simple message: *I'm back, old friend.*

As DeGraff moved through the long corridor, he gazed at aquariums set in the walls. Most were cracked and chipped and covered in mold and moss, their once-captive inhabitants free to roam the building. Cocoons and stringy moss dangled from a high ceiling.

Bugs and lizards covered the walls, the floor, the ceiling. Plump-bodied spiders crawled along the aquariums, millipedes squirmed through gaping cracks in the glass, and scorpions scurried about. Snails dragged themselves along, trails of slime marking their paths. Winged bugs flew in circles, bouncing off one another. As DeGraff walked, he stepped though cobwebs and his boots crunched down on the hard shells of beetles and other unnameable things.

Thinking of the traps set throughout the halls, the corners of his mouth curled with another attempt at a smile. He was ready for them to come. He'd had a year to prepare.

At the entrance of a branching corridor, a door stood coated in bugs. In the outside world, a similar corridor in Creepy Critters was called Bugs-A-Bunch, but DeGraff rarely thought of it by name here. He gripped the handle and a few slow-to-move slugs burst beneath his fingers. Flinging the door open, he stepped inside, the mangy thing-that-had-once-been-a-bear following.

In this corridor, the dirt walls between the aquariums resembled those of a cave. A few flickering torches provided the only light. Hordes of snakelike insects squirmed along the hard floor, occasionally dropping down into the dirty fur of the bear—or the thing which had once been one.

As DeGraff passed a torch, his shadow was cast onto the wall. The dark spot lost its form and took a shape independent of his own. It skimmed the walls, churning the loose dirt and knocking down insects like the slow sweep of a broom.

When DeGraff reached the end of an aisle lined with fish-filled aquariums, he stepped into the Creepy Core, a large, circular room capped with a high, concrete dome. The air stank of mildew, mold, and decay. In the middle of the room stood a man. His hair and eyebrows were bright red, and his face was splotchy with freckles: Charlie Red, once a security guard from the Clarksville Zoo.

In the ground behind Charlie was a deep pit closed off with glass. Four people were far below, Tank and three teenage Descenders, Secret Cityzens who had just been captured by the Shadowist. They were still unconscious, lying on the dirt floor with their arms and legs stretched out. Hannah's long, red-dyed bangs covered her face like a mask, and a few bugs were crawling over her bare feet. The fair skin of Sam's cheeks was bloodied, and Tameron's and Tank's dark skin was streaked with mud.

At Charlie's feet lay a bundle of clothes and equipment—jackets, boots, a hat, a backpack. It was the gear that gave the Descenders their magical strength.

"We got 'em," Charlie said.

DeGraff kept quiet. A small swarm of mosquitoes landed on his face, fed on the poison of his blood, and dropped lifelessly to the ground. He scanned the captives in the pit, then kicked softly through their belongings at Charlie's feet. The thing-that-had-once-been-a-bear sniffed the canvas backpack.

"Not all of them," he answered at last. His rumbly, wet-sounding voice seemed to come from a part of his body that was barely working. "Are the portals closed?"

Charlie nodded. "All but the main entrance into the City of Species."

"Excellent." DeGraff smiled his vile smile. "Darby and his minions—they'll be coming soon. The message has been delivered." The Shadowist wrung his hands together, spreading sticky snail guts across his leather gloves. "Keep watch on the prisoners, Mr. Red. I'll check on our team."

"Yes, sir," Charlie said.

The Shadowist turned and touched the mangy, broad head of the thing-that-had-once-been-a-bear. "Come," he said. "Let's go find your friends."